Terry Overton

Sabal Palms
after
the Storm

Sabal Palms
BOOK TWO

AMBASSADOR INTERNATIONAL
GREENVILLE, SOUTH CAROLINA & BELFAST, NORTHERN IRELAND

www.ambassador-international.com

Sabal Palms After the Storm

ISBN: 978-1-64960-316-6
eISBN: 978-1-64960-355-5
Library of Congress Control Number: 2022937290

Cover design by Hannah Linder Designs
Interior typesetting by Dentelle Design
Edited by Katie Cruice Smith

AMBASSADOR INTERNATIONAL
Emerald House
411 University Ridge, Suite B14
Greenville, SC 29601
United States
www.ambassador-international.com

AMBASSADOR BOOKS
The Mount
2 Woodstock Link
Belfast, BT6 8DD
Northern Ireland, United Kingdom
www.ambassadormedia.co.uk

The colophon is a trademark of Ambassador, a Christian publishing company.

Chapter One

Each morning you get out of bed, not suspecting for one moment that on this particular day, everything you have ever known will change. You could never imagine your life, and the lives of countless other people, would be transformed as a result of your actions and the Divine intervention of a hurricane. This was exactly what had happened a year ago today for Elaine Smith, whose little-known writing had suddenly exploded onto the literary world. You see, Elaine used an old-fashioned typewriter to create devotionals and Christian articles. She believed her writing was not good enough to be read by others, so she tossed the crumpled pieces of paper into the trash container beside her desk. One year ago, God had used a hurricane to send His messages, typed by Elaine's hands, to people who needed to hear them most.

The upheaval and near-complete destruction of Elaine's small Texas coastal town of Sabal Palms had taken only a few hours on that fateful day. Hurricane Jada, a Cat 3 storm, had barreled through the town, leaving no home or building untouched. Today, the blue tarps that covered damaged surviving rooftops were gone. For nearly twelve months, the coastal region of South Texas was abuzz with saws, trucks, and heavy equipment. The homes along the beach had been repaired or rebuilt, and the residents there, including the newly published author

Elaine Smith, were going about their ordinary routines, unaware of a far greater devastation emerging on the horizon.

"Bella, come on, girl," Elaine called to her rescued miniature schnauzer. Bella had been abandoned on the beach after the storm, and Elaine had adopted her right away. The little dog scampered up the beach house steps, wagging her nub of a tail, and lapped up the water in her bowl on the deck.

"Okay, little one, I'll get your breakfast. Then it's down to business. I have a phone conference soon."

Bella wagged her tail faster and turned her head a touch.

Elaine's extensive "to do" list for today replayed over in her mind as she opened the screened door. *First things first,* she thought. *Phone conference with Billy and the record producer, then planning for next steps on the album.*

Since 3:30 a.m., Elaine had been awake worrying about the telephone conference with her collaborative songwriter, Billy Wrangle, and their producer in Nashville. In her mind, she reviewed the topics to cover during the conference. The disturbing sound of footsteps crunching on the seashell walkway interrupted her thoughts. Her plans for the day were about to be upended.

"Oh! There you are!" Bonnie yelled.

"Here I am." Elaine stopped in her tracks, unsure how Bonnie was about to disrupt her day.

Appearing at the top of the steps dressed in her white capris, sea foam green top, and matching sandals, Bonnie said, "I missed you when you walked by my house earlier. You did walk by?"

Looking at Bonnie, Elaine noticed she was far too dressy for a casual day at her own beach house. "Yes, I did come by earlier today."

"Didn't see you. Guess I was getting dressed."

Bella launched toward Bonnie and licked her ankles.

"Oh!" Bonnie sighed. "And here *you* are, pooch."

After Elaine rescued Bella, Bonnie wasted no time letting her feelings be known about the dog to anyone within earshot. She tolerated the little dog, but in truth, she had no use for her.

"What's up, Bonnie? Going somewhere?" Elaine asked, tiring of the suspense.

"You forgot," Bonnie declared.

"Forgot?"

"You're taking me into town for my lab test results."

"Oh, no! I *did* forget. It will just take me a minute to get changed. I'll drive you over. Come in if you like."

Bonnie followed Elaine up the steps and into the cottage. Bonnie looked at her watch. "This is a fine how-do-you-do. I'm supposed to be there in twenty-minutes."

Elaine found a pair of capris and a summer top in record speed. "Okay. Almost ready."

It had been years since Bonnie's husband, Bill, had died. Shortly after his death, Bonnie had sold the car. Although Elaine prayed Bonnie would buy her own car, it was evident Elaine would continue to be Bonnie's taxi for an undetermined length of time.

Elaine's mind was tangled up with thoughts of the phone conference with Billy Wrangle and the interference of this last-minute ride into town. How could she have forgotten Bonnie's annual lab results? Why did she schedule the conference call on the same day as Bonnie's doctor's appointment? How would she be able to have a Zoom conference call while driving? "That's what happens when you don't put it on your calendar," she mumbled, fussing at herself.

"Slippage," she murmured.

This term, *slippage,* was rarely, if ever, discussed among her best friends. In fact, Mary, Bonnie, Adriana, and Elaine herself never, under *any* circumstances, brought it up. It was as off-limits as arm wrinkles and thigh cellulite when the women were in their swimsuits. If mentioned, the word *slippage* was promptly hushed over faster than butter melts in a hot skillet. *Slippage* was defined by the women as the slow ebbing away of one's ability to use short-term memory. They used the word when speaking of others; but never, ever, ever would this word be used in reference to or as a direct question about the four women themselves. All four of the women increasingly relied on notes, calendars, and kindly reminders to each other of important events, such as church gatherings, cookouts on the beach, or pool parties at Adriana's. And today was a perfect example of why Elaine needed a calendar, and, more importantly, she needed to *use* it. Double-booking or flat-out forgetting events was avoided for fear that the term *slippage* might be uttered.

It took five minutes for Elaine to change from her walking shorts to presentable clothes. "Okay. Ready." Elaine grabbed her car keys and headed for the front door.

***

Driving into town presented another opportunity for the women to see the latest "For Sale," "Sale Pending," and "Sold" realtor signs scattered along the road. The turnover of property was astronomical after Hurricane Jada. Homeowners actively battled for curb-appeal and a share of market attention. The newly planted palm trees and oleanders were cleverly placed in award-winning landscaped lawns for each rebuilt or repaired house. Renovated homes lined the road, begging for new owners. When an owner was contacted by a realtor to schedule a showing of the property to a potential buyer, the word spread faster than the rising tide in a tidal flat.

In disbelief, Elaine shook her head. "Can you believe what's happened to Sabal Palms since last year?"

"No. Droves of people anxious to leave, saying they wouldn't go through another storm. Fools! Selling so cheap! I would never—"

"Now, Bonnie, not everyone is meant to stay here on the coast. They like being inland. Maybe they feel safer."

"Chickens! Seriously! They will move someplace even worse! They will end up in a location where there are tornados! Or fires! Or earthquakes. Oh, for heaven's sakes! Selling their homes after a simple storm!" she barked.

As the volume of her voice increased, so did the redness of Bonnie's face. Elaine glanced at Bonnie's crimson countenance. "Bonnie, I'm curious. Will the nurse be taking your blood pressure when you check in at the doctor's office?"

Grumbling, she muttered, "Oh . . . okay." Bonnie closed her eyes and took deep breaths to calm down.

"Anyway, Bonnie, what's so awful about new people moving in? It could bring some excitement to our little town."

"Excitement? You're kidding, right? Wait. You're *not* kidding! Have you already forgotten the excitement brought on by your writing after the hurricane? And how we must now hide your true identity? Someday, someone will find out your real name. Then there will be no privacy, no quiet, little strip of beach in front of our cottages. We will be overrun by paparazzi! Tourists wanting autographs! Crowding us everywhere! Can you even imagine? Whoever thought of your pen name, Terry Overton, anyway? What kind of cockamamie name is that? Sounds like a man's name. Terry—with a *y*? Someone will find out, and then what? Probably one of those new people moving in will discover who you really are. They will try to change everything! They will be a bunch of nosy busybodies—"

"About your blood pressure?'

Bonnie grumbled something Elaine couldn't hear, folded her arms, and sat in silence the rest of the way as the car meandered down the small road to town. Nearing town, Bonnie murmured, "Well, for the love of Pete. Look at Mr. McGregor."

Glancing to the right side of the road, Elaine noticed Mr. McGregor pulling his trash can to the curb. "Wonder why he is doing that? It's not trash pick-up for two more days."

"I wonder . . ." Bonnie said quietly. "I wonder if it's . . . Could it be slippage?"

"Heaven forbid," Elaine whispered.

Elaine turned the last corner on the route and parked the car. Bonnie opened her door, then looked at Elaine before stepping out. "Well, at least I won't have to put on that foolish tissue paper gown for this appointment. Just about freeze to death in those things. You coming inside?"

"No. I'll wait here. I need to contact Billy this morning."

"Okay. The results of my tests shouldn't take long. Waiting to get in to see the doctor for my appointment, now that's a different story," she said with a huff and closed the car door.

"I'll be here when you finish."

Elaine texted Billy to let him know she would have to reschedule their video conference call with Nashville. He answered back right away and assured her their producer would understand. He suggested they reschedule for tomorrow. Elaine sent a quick thank you back to him.

How did I get myself into this? I'm retired, she thought.

She paused for a moment. She knew exactly how she had ended up in a deal with Billy Wrangle and the record company. It was her own writing that had paved the way. The words of her story were used by Billy in his first hit song. Her thoughts carried her back to the day when he said, "Your words saved my life. I was at the end, at the bottom—rock bottom—and your writing saved me." Her written words, lost somehow on a scrap of paper in Hurricane Jada, were found by Billy Wrangle and had made a difference to him. He was able to survive the heartbreak of his fiancée's tragic death. He was back on his feet and planned to bring Elaine right along with him on his musical rise to the top.

This thought brought a smile to her face. She nodded and whispered, "My writing made a difference to Billy. That's how I got here." She remembered the other people who had found her scraps of paper with her devotionals and how her words had helped them. Jack had found her passages, as had Cara, and then there was—

Elaine was so lost in her thoughts, she didn't see Bonnie walking toward the car, and the opening of the car door startled her.

Alarmed by Bonnie's red face and current state of mind, she said, "Oh, Bonnie, sorry, I wasn't paying . . . Bonnie, are you okay?"

Bonnie whimpered a bit, blew her nose, and then sat in the car and closed the door.

"Bonnie?"

"Stupid tests."

"Bonnie, what is it?" Elaine placed her hand on Bonnie's shoulder.

"I'm getting old." She sniffled.

"But is everything okay? Your tests—were they okay?"

She sniffled again and wiped her eyes. "My glucose. It's borderline."

"Oh? What does that mean?"

Bonnie buried her face in her hands and began to cry. She was in a full-blown bawling episode. She was inconsolable.

"Bonnie, Bonnie, now, it's okay. We'll figure this all out." She patted Bonnie's hand. "How about we go over to Mary's house for a cup of coffee?"

Bonnie wiped her nose and nodded.

Elaine texted Mary and then started the engine.

Bonnie didn't say another word. She opened her purse and took out two pieces of paper. She stared at the pages for the remaining six blocks to Mary's house. In all the years Elaine had known Bonnie, she had never been so quiet. She wasn't this quiet even when Bill had passed away.

Elaine parked her car. She and Bonnie opened their car doors and saw Mary dressed in her blue "Save the Manatees" t-shirt and a pair of shorts waving from her porch.

"Come on up, girls. I just put on a fresh pot of coffee."

Elaine stepped out of the car and gave Mary the "I don't know" shoulder shrug. Bonnie quietly got out of the car and walked up the steps to the large, sprawling, Southern front porch. Elaine and Bonnie took their seats in the wicker rocking chairs.

Ignoring Bonnie's silence, Mary remarked, "Good to see the two of you. I was just thinking we haven't had a morning coffee in a while. I'll get the coffee and fixin's."

Mary returned with a beautiful wicker tray full of coffee, dainty dishes, napkins, and sweet rolls. Bonnie took one look at the array of pastries and burst into tears.

"Oh, dear. Honey, what's wrong?" Mary asked.

Bonnie blew her nose again—this time, a long, honking blow into her tissue. She wiped her eyes and said, "It's my blood sugar. I can't . . . I can't eat sugar."

"Oh, dear me." Mary's wide eyes turned to Elaine in shock.

This would be a whole change of lifestyle for Bonnie and Mary, whose very lives were centered on pies, cakes, and cooking in general. The essence of all social gatherings had always been food.

"Here, sweetie, take some coffee." Mary handed Bonnie a cup and the cream. "Now, now, it might not be so bad. Tell us exactly what you found out."

Bonnie sighed. "I'm borderline diabetic. The doctor said my glucose has been inching up over the years. And now, my fasting blood sugar"—she sniffed again—"was 107." Her whimpers turned to tears.

"Goodness," Mary said. "What in the world is it supposed to be?"

Trying to compose herself, she murmured, "Under one hundred."

"I see." Mary put her hand on Bonnie's arm. "Now, that isn't so bad. Just a little over one hundred."

Bonnie semi-collected herself. "I can't eat carbs. I can't eat grains. I can't eat sugar." She whimpered and wiped her eyes. "What is a carb, anyway? What is left? What *can* I eat?"

Mary, known for having no verbal filter whatsoever, blurted out, "Salad. Oh, and meat. Guess that's all that's left. Lettuce and meat."

Elaine looked at Bonnie's face to detect the reaction. The inaccurate statement that Bonnie would be restricted to eat only meat and green salad might cause Bonnie to go into a fit of rage. Elaine expected an emotional explosion or breakdown any second.

Bonnie was unexpectedly calm. "Well"—she sniffed and wiped her nose—"what *is* a carb?"

Once again, Mary revealed the truth too quickly. "Potatoes, bread, rice—you know, all the good stuff."

Bonnie sobbed again, but a little quieter.

Elaine shot Mary a disapproving look. If she had been sitting beside Mary, she would have elbowed her. "Bonnie, what did the doctor tell you to do?"

Holding up a piece of paper, Bonnie mumbled, "She said to follow this diet. Low carb, no sugar. And to . . . " She sniffed again, threatening another good cry. The tears were about to spout like Niagara Falls.

"What, dear?" Mary asked.

And now, the full-blown cry happened again. In the middle of her sobbing, she muttered, "Exercise and . . . " More sobbing. "I have to test my sugar . . . every . . . morning." She was sobbing nonstop by the time she blubbered out the last two words.

"What? Why every morning? You aren't diabetic. For Pete's sakes, why?" Mary shrieked.

"To see if"—she sniffed again and wiped her eyes—"if I can get my sugar lower by eating on this diet."

With no advance notice or invitation, Adriana, the youngest and wealthiest of the four women, pulled into the driveway and honked the horn of her red sports car.

"Hey, girls," she shouted. The jangling of her jewelry could be heard from the driveway when she waved. "I was on my way to the store and—" Adriana glanced across the porch and saw Bonnie's current state of total meltdown. "Wait, what is happening? What's the matter?"

Elaine stood up and gestured to Adriana. "Come on up."

Adriana turned off her car and joined the women on the porch. At times like this, these women all pulled together. They had been through worse scenarios. They had helped each other through the Category Three hurricane just last year. They had supported each other when their husbands had passed away. They were at Adriana's side when she had found out her husband, Antony, was murdered by the mobster Frankie the Gun. They would get through this, too. They would help Bonnie pull through and come out on the other side healthier than ever.

Bonnie, Mary, and Elaine brought Adriana up to speed on what was happening, including the details of the diet Bonnie was allowed to eat.

Adriana, being the proud and very dramatic Italian—Sicilian, to be exact—that she was, waved her hands in the air with her sparkling bracelets flashing around, and gasped, "Oh my! No pasta? No bread? I couldn't do it! I just couldn't! Oh, Bonnie!"

Elaine shot Adriana a look.

Bonnie burst into tears once again.

Elaine sensed the need to reign in Bonnie's panic and Adriana's frenzied reaction. "I'm sure we will all do our part to help Bonnie find the kind of recipes she will need. We can learn to cook some dishes and help her out. It won't hurt for us to improve our own health."

Taking another tissue from her purse, Bonnie managed a meager smile. "You would do that?"

It took Mary a few moments to process Bonnie's earlier comments. Then she turned to Bonnie in shock. "Oh, my word! Bonnie, do you have to stick your finger every day to test your sugar? Oh, my goodness! *Every* day?"

This initiated another full-blown crying episode.

Elaine was exasperated. At times, there was just *no* controlling Mary. She must redirect the whole conversation. "Bonnie, I have an idea."

Still bawling, Bonnie looked at Elaine.

Louder, Elaine announced, "Girls, I have an idea."

All eyes focused on Elaine. "I know what we can do. I will search online and order us different cookbooks for this diet—this low-carb, no-sugar thing. We can do this." Elaine wanted Mary and Adriana to settle down, and she wanted Bonnie to think positively. "We will do this together." But at times like this, it was difficult to console even your best friend.

Bonnie calmed a bit. Mary took the sweet rolls back into the house and out of sight. Adriana hugged Bonnie and provided sympathetic looks.

After a few moments, Bonnie collected herself, smoothed her hair, and straightened her blouse.

"Bonnie, what would you like to do now?" Elaine asked.

She unfolded the instructional papers from the doctor. "I need to go to the drugstore and get this."

Elaine took the papers from Bonnie and read the instructions for monitoring fasting glucose. "Well, then, we'll go to the drugstore before we go home. Then once you and I are back at our cottages, we will go for a nice, long walk on the beach. That will be a first step to increase your exercise. We'll walk at least twice a day on the beach. Easy for us to do that. We'll put on our shorts and flip-flops and get going." Then, with a voice of authority, Elaine added, "And girls, tonight, cookout at my place. It will be our first healthy meal on our new road to get this thing under control."

Mary and Adriana nodded.

Bonnie managed a meager smile. She gathered her papers and placed them in her purse.

Elaine smiled at her successful effort to turn this crying jag around. "All right, then. We will gather at my house at 5:30 this afternoon. I'll look up a few recipes online and text each of you to let you know what to bring."

Mary, once again spouting off before she thought it through, asked, "But what about dessert?"

"Mary!" Adriana roared, throwing up her arms and rattling her jewelry.

"No, no, don't worry," Elaine said. "I will find something we will all eat and enjoy."

Bonnie stood up and nodded to Elaine. "I'm ready. Let's go to the drugstore and get this over with."

Chapter Two

The number of available cookbooks for this new, healthy-eating lifestyle overwhelmed Elaine. She scrolled through the options online and selected four cookbooks, one for each of her best friends and one for her. She ordered the whole bundle of cookbooks to be delivered by express to her house, so they would arrive on the same day. She planned to have another get-together in a few days to disperse the books and plan menus.

A basic book would work for Adriana with an emphasis on low-carb pasta and breads. Cooking was never a favorite activity for Adriana, who preferred eating elsewhere, usually at the homes of the other three women. And for Bonnie and herself, she selected the two most comprehensive sugar-free, low-carb cookbooks. Each of these comprehensive cookbooks included basic explanations of Bonnie's medical issues. The final cookbook selection, one on sugar-free, low-carb desserts, was for Mary, who, like Bonnie, was known for her award-winning confections.

"There," she announced to Bella after she hit the payment button on the website shopping cart. "All done." Bella wagged her tail.

Next, Elaine searched online for simple but tasty recipes for the cookout. She saved a few side dish recipes in a new file folder she named "Compliant recipes." She emailed those to Mary and Adriana for the side dishes, then texted each one and told them to check their email. She didn't send any recipes to Bonnie. Bonnie needed to be entertained tonight. Elaine would ease her into this change of lifestyle.

At precisely 5:30 p.m., Bonnie was first on the steps to the deck.

Elaine gestured as she called out, "Hey, come on up and check out these shrimp kabobs."

Bonnie's eyes zoomed in on the bacon-wrapped jumbo shrimp skewered between red and green bell peppers and mushrooms. "Those look amazing!" Bonnie said.

Good. Her spirits are better, Elaine thought.

"And wait until you see what we are having for dessert."

Bonnie smiled.

Mary, as predictable as the tropical sunset, was the second to reach Elaine's deck followed by the always-fashionably-late Adriana.

"Oh, my goodness!" Adriana gushed walking up the steps.

The three women's heads turned to see what Adriana, who relied on the use of dramatic hand gesturing as an integral part of communication, would announce this time.

Waving her arms around, Adriana repeated, "Oh, my goodness!"

"Well, spill it," Mary demanded.

"Do you know what I heard at the farmer's market today?"

"How could we know? We weren't with you." Mary chuckled causing her dangling turtle earrings to swing back and forth.

Adriana ignored Mary's comment. "I heard that a new, *very* wealthy developer is moving to Sabal Palms. A guy with *piles* of money, moving *here!*"

Mary rolled her eyes, "Oh, here we go. Some new guy will probably want to change everything!"

"It could be just fine. Maybe he wants to, you know, improve the downtown district—put in new lights, benches, and update the landscaping a bit," Elaine reasoned.

"That's a possibility." Bonnie smiled.

"Can you imagine? Oh! That would be wonderful! A new look for our old little town. Maybe he will put in some new shops, stores, or . . . " Adriana gasped. "Oh! A mall!"

Elaine noticed Bonnie's increasing agitation at Adriana's dramatics. Mary's entire face frowned. "Oh, horsefeathers! Who wants a mall? We can drive over to McAllen or Brownsville or Harlingen for a stinkin' mall! For Pete's sakes! Think of the traffic! I like having no traffic and only one traffic signal in town!"

Practically bubbling with excitement, Adriana disagreed, "I think it would be grand! With stores of all kinds—boutique clothing stores, jewelry stores, specialty shops, and, well, everything! Oh, and, Elaine, a bookstore!"

Elaine knew the afterthought bookstore comment was an effort to win Elaine over to her side of the argument. There was no way Elaine would support the idea of a mall, but she kept the conversation going to serve as a distraction from Bonnie's health issue.

"A bookstore would be nice," Elaine acknowledged.

"Oh phooey! He probably wants to put in a high-rise condominium complex like those on the island!" Mary insisted. "We will be slammed with tourists! It's all a bunch of poppycock if you ask me! Who does he think he is?"

"Mary, we have no clue who he is! Good grief! We don't know his name or anything about him. But I can't imagine our quiet, little community with a high-rise! Ridiculous!" Bonnie grimaced. "After all, Sabal Palms is the little, hidden gem on the shore! 'The Tropical Tip of Texas,' as they say. The best kept secret on the Southern coast."

Shaking her finger at her friends, Adriana insisted, "That ship has sailed! I don't think it's a secret anymore. Being a feature story on the news and weather for so long after Jada, we are known by everyone in the entire world. The word is out."

"Yes, and these people with tons of money believe they can swoop down here and get something pristine and cheap right on the beach," Bonnie said. "Outrageous!"

Elaine wanted to switch the conversation. Bonnie had been through enough today. She had ridden an emotional roller coaster. "Oh! I almost forgot to tell you. Billy will be here next week. He has another song for the album he wants us to work on together. And we could plan a welcome-back party!"

Adriana jumped on board immediately. She loved all the glamor surrounding the new hit country singer. "Yes! Let's do it!" Adriana's hands were moving around faster than her lips at this point. "Great idea! I love it! We could have a party at my pool—"

"I would love to host a party on my expanded deck watching the sunset," Bonnie interrupted.

Knowing the kind of day Bonnie had, Elaine believed Bonnie should have the honor of hosting the party. If Bonnie was enthused, it was a good sign she would focus on the party for the next week.

Elaine agreed. "That would be great for a large welcome-back gathering on your oversized deck. Billy will be here for a month. Adriana, you could host a more intimate pool party later."

"Perfect!" Adriana said. "A pool party for a small guest list! I love it."

With a single clap of her hands, Elaine said, "Good. It's settled. Next week, a welcome-back party at Bonnie's, and a week or so later, Adriana's pool party."

***

Clean-up was easy after the cookout. The women pitched in and finished in no time. "Those kabobs! Elaine, you just outdid yourself!" Adriana declared. "And those jumbo shrimp! Did you get them at Joe's Seafood Market?"

Elaine nodded. "Yes, I did. In Port Isabel. He has the best seafood. And thank you, Mary, for bringing the deviled eggs to go with it. And Adriana, that salad with those toasted almonds on top was very tasty."

"Thank you," Adriana smiled.

"Now, ladies, should we go walk on the beach and look at this amazing sunset that is about to happen? And when we get back, I'll serve you all a surprise dessert."

The women agreed and set off, with Bella tagging along sniffing for crabs under the sand and chasing the seagulls and sandpipers. The sky was filled with splashes of orange and pink streaks, and the red-orange sun slowly lowered behind the cottages along the beach. There was just enough of a sea breeze off the water to sway the onshore palm trees. It was a beautiful, late summer evening.

Adriana pointed to the sky. "What a *treat*! Look at this moon. It's going to be *beautiful* shimmering above the water when the sky is darker."

"The bright moon over the water." Bonnie nodded. "What a sight!"

The women returned to Elaine's beach cottage in a calmer mood with no mention of the mysterious new developer or condominiums or malls.

"Okay, ladies, have a seat at the kitchen table, and I'll bring out a treat."

Bonnie's eyes brightened up a bit. She loved baking and making all kinds of desserts, but she loved eating them even more.

Elaine opened the refrigerator and took out four small, ice-cream-sized dishes. Each dish was full of strawberries with a dollop of whipped cream on the top.

"What? I can eat this?"

"Yes. As a matter of fact, this is the recommended amount of berries, and the whipped cream is made with a sprinkle of a healthier type of sugar substitute and a touch of vanilla."

"Seriously? This is healthy?" Bonnie asked with disbelief.

Elaine handed each of the women a dessert spoon and replied, "Yes. Taste it."

Adriana waved her hands in the air and said, "Oh! Oh! This is amazing!"

Words were replaced by "oohs" and "ahs" as the women finished their desserts.

Although Bonnie was feeling better, Elaine feared tomorrow. Bonnie would be pricking her own finger for the first time, and that might be reason enough for Bonnie's spirits to tank once again.

The women helped Elaine clear up dessert dishes and said their farewells. Elaine wanted to be there for Bonnie in the morning, just in case. That's what friends do.

"Bonnie, how about I come over in the morning? We can eat breakfast and go for a walk on the beach?"

"Sounds good to me." Bonnie then did something unexpected and out of character. She hugged Elaine and said, "Thank you for being such a good friend. And that dessert was such a great surprise! I can survive this diet! I can do this!"

Surprised by Bonnie's sudden display of affection, Elaine hugged Bonnie right back. "You're welcome." She hoped Bonnie would remain positive as they tackled this new chapter in her life.

"Come over around 6:30 then?" Bonnie asked.

"Sure. I'm up by then, so I will see you bright and early."

Bonnie left for her beach cottage. Elaine closed the screen door and heard Adriana and Mary start their cars and drive away. She promptly sat at her desk and began to write. She placed the clean piece of paper in her trusty, old typewriter and rolled it to the correct position. She hoped her devotional would be meaningful—maybe she would give it to Bonnie someday.

"This will be a devotional about friendship," she said to herself.

Bella wagged her tail and found her fuzzy, little bed beside the desk. Bella knew when a routine writing session was about to begin.

Elaine typed right up until midnight, then called it a day. Six a.m. would arrive quickly.

***

The sun was just peeking out on the water at 6:15 a.m. Elaine looked down at Bella, who was waiting patiently for breakfast. "I'll get your food, Bella." Elaine put the dogfood in a baggie, picked up her housekey, and walked to the front door. "Okay, girl, we're eating breakfast at Bonnie's today. Let's go."

Bella ran behind Elaine on the beach and darted toward the waves rolling up, then ran away before the waves caught the pooch.

Bonnie was out on the deck when Elaine and Bella arrived.

"Good morning. Looks like you are eager this morning," Elaine said.

"Yes. Glad you're out early. I'm hungry but need to test my blood sugar before I can eat. I've been waiting for you. I'm starving!"

"Me, too," Elaine agreed. "Do you have a little plate or bowl I can use to feed Bella?"

"Sure do."

Inside, Elaine saw the blood sugar test items waiting on the counter. As soon as Bella was fed and back out on the deck, Elaine asked, "Well, are you ready? Then we can get breakfast cooking."

"Oh, for heaven's sakes, let's just get it done."

Elaine read the instructions to Bonnie, and she followed along. And then she did it. She stuck her own finger and placed the sample on the test strip and into the meter. The meter beeped and flashed a number.

"That's not so bad. But have to say I didn't think I'd be spending my last years doing this every day."

"What is it?"

"What is what?"

"The number?"

"Oh, well, will you look at that! It's ninety-nine!"

"See? You're already going in the right direction!"

Bonnie smiled. "Yes! Good. Now, how about bacon and eggs? Oh, no toast today, though."

"Bacon and eggs sound wonderful. Then, a nice, long, early walk."

"That's a plan."

Elaine was proud of Bonnie, although she feared Bonnie might be putting on a show to cover up her sadness about dealing with her lifelong medical issue. Elaine's own mother had diabetes, and it upset her mother quite a bit. But Elaine intended to help Bonnie to prevent the same outcome, if possible.

Finishing her last bite of eggs, Elaine asked, "You want to walk down to the church? It's a little further than our usual walk."

Bonnie nodded. "Of course. We have plenty of time for a long walk. And I am supposed to increase my exercise."

Bonnie insisted the dirty dishes could wait, so they could be on their way to the church. Bella followed the two women ambling and talking the entire distance on the beach. The breeze was light, and the sun wasted no time heating up the morning air.

"Elaine, can you believe what Adriana told us? About a developer moving here?"

"I was shocked. It was the first I'd heard about it. Sabal Palms is still recovering from Jada. I imagine this developer found some very reasonably priced land."

"You mean cheap. Just say it. Cheap, not reasonably priced. People seem to be scrambling to leave. I don't understand how people who have lived here all of their lives are now suddenly just throwing in the towel."

Elaine shook her head. "I couldn't do it. I moved inland once. Never again."

"Absurd. And what I said before, you just watch. Those people who move away will find themselves in tornado alley or sitting on top of a major fault line; and then their new homes will be split in two, or they will buy property by a river that floods, or a wildfire area will go up in smoke, or a mudslide that will wash them away—"

"Oh, Bonnie!"

They walked faster as Bonnie became more animated. Shrugging her shoulders, she continued, "What? Why would they want to move anywhere else? Absurd! Chickens, I tell you."

"Beats me why they would move. Oh, look, there, at the church," Elaine pointed. "There must be a meeting going on."

Parked outside the small beachside church were ten cars.

Elaine knew Bonnie was not about to ignore this unexplained event. She would get to the bottom of anything newsworthy.

"Something is definitely happening. Now, what can it be? Can't be a funeral. Nobody died. There wouldn't be a wedding this early in the morning. Good grief. Why didn't we hear something was happening today?"

"Do you recognize any of the cars?" Elaine asked. If anyone knew who drove which car in Sabal Palms, Bonnie did. It was hard to distinguish who knew more about the comings and goings in town— Bonnie or Adriana.

"Looks like Elizabeth Randolph's car, and that one is Mark Carter's truck. That's it!" Bonnie exclaimed.

"What?"

"It's an executive committee meeting. Some of those people work, and I'll bet they had to squeeze the meeting in before work hours. That means it's not a routine meeting. Something's up. This has the look of an emergency meeting. Wait, I hope nothing is wrong with Pastor Sam. Oh, where is Adriana when we need her? She always knows everything about everyone's business in Sabal Palms."

By the time the two women reached the church, a few people were walking to their cars. The meeting was over. Most of the executive committee members drove away, but Elizabeth Randolph, lagging behind the others, stepped out from the front door of the church onto the porch.

"Let's ask her," Bonnie said.

"She might be uncomfortable."

"Why?" Bonnie asked.

"The meeting might be secret."

"Oh, baloney! I'm going to ask her." Bonnie marched toward the parking lot. "Hey, Elizabeth!" Bonnie waved. "Elizabeth!"

Looking as if she wanted to escape, Elizabeth reluctantly stopped and waited for Bonnie and Elaine.

"Good morning, ladies," Elisabeth said.

"What's new?" Bonnie asked. "Something must be going on."

"Oh, our executive committee meeting just ended. How are you, ladies?"

"Fine," Elaine answered.

"Elizabeth, what was the meeting about? I thought your group met on Saturday afternoon."

"That's right. Unless we have a reason. Something came up."

"Well, what?" Bonnie pressed.

Elaine felt Elizabeth's reluctance. It was clear Elizabeth wanted to keep the purpose of the meeting to herself. Elaine knew Bonnie wouldn't stand for it. Elizabeth might as well surrender every last nanobyte of information. Elaine figured Bonnie would wait until she heard every detail.

Bonnie continued to stare directly at Elizabeth until the poor woman must have felt besieged and had no choice but to relinquish the executive meeting word by word.

"Oh, phooey. You'll find out soon enough, anyway. I might as well tell you. Pastor Sam is leaving."

"What? What are you talking about?" Bonnie asked.

"He received a call to a larger church in a city by his family."

"That's understandable," Elaine said.

"How could he?" Bonnie demanded. "This church has grown so much with Pastor Sam. Are you certain? Can't we ask him to change his mind?"

Elizabeth said, "He has given us his letter of resignation. Said that Jada made him rethink his options."

"For goodness' sakes!" Bonnie said. "Another one chased off by Jada!"

Eager to help Elizabeth escape further questioning, Elaine said, "Thank you, Elizabeth. Bonnie, shall we go back?"

Chapter Three

The cookbooks arrived in two days. Elaine notified Bonnie and Adriana that a last-minute dinner would be served at her house. She was able, at last, to reach Mary, who had been volunteering for two days at the South Padre Island Birding Center. Elaine asked them to each bring along paper or notebooks—whatever they wanted to use to plan out some menus. As it turned out, the conversation was dominated by something other than cooking that evening.

"Hey! Elaine!" Adriana yelled from her car as she drove into Elaine's driveway.

"Adriana, you're first to arrive. How did you beat Mary and Bonnie over here? You never beat them."

"Oh, my goodness! I couldn't wait to tell you! Just wait till you hear this!" She threw her hands in the air, her bracelets glimmering in the sun.

Before Adriana could spurt out her latest gossip from town, Mary and Bonnie arrived.

"Adriana, you're here early," Mary said. "Anxious about something?"

"Yes. I left as soon as I heard the latest, and then, well, I met him."

"Who?" Mary asked.

"The developer. The new guy. The guy with all the money."

"Wait! What? You did? Where? How?" Mary asked.

"What does he look like? Is he nice?" Bonnie asked. "Or does he look like someone who is here to take advantage of our little town?"

"Does he look like a swindler?" Mary blurted.

This situation was about to blow up, and Elaine feared they wouldn't get down to the important business of the night if the gossip continued. "Hold on a minute. Let's go inside, and I'll show you what arrived today."

"I can't stand the suspense, Elaine. Adriana, you have to tell us!" Mary insisted.

"Okay, well . . . " Then Adriana glanced at Elaine. "Oh, I'm sorry, Elaine. It's your dinner party. Let's go inside, and I will tell you all in a little while." Adriana winked and walked up the shell path to Elaine's beach cottage.

With disappointment on Bonnie and Mary's faces, they went along with the plan and followed Elaine into the house.

Elaine dispensed the cookbooks, and the women thumbed through each one.

"These are wonderful," Bonnie said. "Look at these beautiful pictures! The pictures are making me hungry! This was so considerate. Thank you for doing this for me."

Mary smiled and added, "Well, it won't hurt the rest of us to eat better. And you know I love to cook. So, I'll just learn some of these new recipes." She patted the new cookbook and looked through the pages.

"These allowable breads and pastas will be terrific! Looks yummy. I can always fix both kinds—the regular and these recipes—and we can take our pick."

Bonnie's face looked quite somber. "I hope you all know how much this means to me that you are going to do this to help me. I wouldn't know what to do without you all. It means a lot. Really, thank you."

The brief silence was interrupted by Mary. "Of course, dear. You would do the same for us."

"This will be an adventure, and we'll do it together," Adriana said. "And you know it probably wouldn't hurt if we all brought our sugar habit under control. I mean, I could eat cakes and pies all day long—might as well eat the healthy kind!"

They laughed and chatted about the cookbooks and pointed to the large, color pictures of each delightful recipe. Elaine talked from the kitchen, where she assembled dinner. She served chef salads with all the trimmings and a variety of healthy dressings.

"Ladies, we need to talk a bit about the menu for Billy's welcome-back party. Bonnie is hosting, but we should help her because it will be a pretty large gathering," Elaine suggested.

"That would be appreciated. Oh, and I invited Pastor Sam and his wife to come, since they will be leaving," Bonnie said.

"What?" Mary asked. "I hadn't heard that."

"You've been off rescuing turtles or whatever," Bonnie said.

"I was at the birding center," Mary quipped.

"Oh, well, anyway, we haven't seen you in the past couple of days to tell you. I'm not sure it's public information yet," Elaine said.

"What happened?" Adriana asked. "And who will replace him?"

Bonnie filled them in on the news Elizabeth Randolph had revealed. Then she added, "We didn't talk about the replacement."

"We were just taken aback by the news. It was sudden," Elaine said.

"For heaven's sakes," Mary said, "all this leaving, moving, selling homes, real estate development—what a mess!"

"Speaking of real estate, Adriana, tell us now. Tell us about the developer. What do you know?" Bonnie asked.

"I met him."

"And?" Mary said.

"Where?" Bonnie asked.

"What does he look like?" Mary asked. "Does he look like a scoundrel? A crook?"

"Did you like him?" Bonnie asked. "And where were you? Where did you meet him? What did he say? What did you say?"

"Girls, slow down, and I will explain. He was in the town office. He came out on to Main Street, and I practically ran into him on the sidewalk. I mean literally! I bumped him! Oh, my goodness, gracious! He looks like a movie star! His eyes twinkle. Honestly, they really do! Twinkle! I kid you not! It's like there were stars in his eyes! I don't think I've ever seen anyone as handsome—well, except poor Antony, God rest his soul." And she made the sign of the cross on her chest as she always did when she talked about her late husband.

"Tell us!" Mary interrupted. "Come on, details."

"He took my hand and said he was sorry and that it was his fault that he ran into me. But of course, it was my fault because I was looking for my lipstick in my purse and didn't see him. I couldn't find my coral shade, so I settled for the pink one—you know, in the mother of pearl case. And that one was, of course, at the very bottom of my purse. Anyway, I looked in those eyes . . . He has the bluest eyes. Oh, my stars!" Adriana took her cookbook and used it to fan her crimson face.

"We get the picture; now, tell us what happened," Mary said.

"He told me his name and asked mine, and I told him. He said how nice it was to meet me and wanted to know a good restaurant in town."

"Was that the end of it? Was that all?" Mary asked.

"Shush! Give her time," Bonnie said. Then she added, "Was that all? Was it the end of it?"

Elaine just shook her head. The evening would not be very productive at the rate they were going. Frustrated, Elaine raised her voice slightly. "Okay. We know the new guy is here. We know that Pastor Sam is leaving. And we know that Billy Wrangle is arriving in three days, and we *need* to plan a party for *next week*. Do you suppose we can get on with it?"

Speechless, the three women looked at Elaine. Elaine, typically very quiet and agreeable, was at her wit's end. For her to spout off so directly was unnatural.

"Elaine, I'm sorry," Bonnie said. "We got carried away. Of course, we're going to plan the party. We're not used to so many changes going on at the same time."

Adriana looked at Elaine apologetically. The room was silent. "I need to add one little, teeny, tiny detail," Adriana pleaded to Elaine.

"Which is?" Mary asked.

"Actually, two details."

"Well?" Bonnie asked.

"First, this very handsome, charming man's name is Trent Fortune—"

"Wait, you *are* kidding! Fortune? You mean, as in money?" Mary laughed.

"I'm not kidding. That is what he said his name is—Trent Fortune."

"Good grief. I never—" Bonnie said.

"Let her finish," Mary insisted. "What is the other detail?"

"Yes, tell us," Bonnie insisted.

"He told me that tomorrow morning, at the town hall meeting room, he will be presenting his proposal for development, and we are all invited. The whole town is invited to see what he wants to do."

Mary huffed, "*That*, ladies, is what is known as burying the lead! The meeting is the most important thing—not that his eyes twinkled, for goodness' sake!"

"That meeting sounds like something we should attend," Elaine said.

"Absolutely," Bonnie agreed. "How about if we meet at Mary's and all go together? What time is the meeting?"

"Ten in the morning."

Mary nodded. "Perfect. You all come over at 8:30 for coffee and one of these healthy breakfast rolls. We can visit more about planning the party and then go over to the meeting. Of course, we can go back to my house afterward and talk about what we learned if you like."

"It's a deal. We'll be over bright and early," Bonnie said.

***

That night, Elaine sat before her typewriter and thought about changes. *Some are good; some are not*, she thought. She knew that either way, it would all be in God's plan.

She thumbed through her Bible. It was always an inspiration to her.

She read aloud to herself, "'*For I know the plans I have for you*, declares the LORD, *plans for welfare and not for evil, to give you a future and a hope*,' Jeremiah 29:11."

Bella wagged her tail and snuggled down into her little bed.

***

Bonnie knocked on Elaine's door at 8:15.

"Come on in, Bonnie. I am just feeding Bella."

"I couldn't sleep all night. I tossed and turned. I tell you; I just couldn't sleep."

"Bonnie, what was the matter? Did you not feel well?"

"Oh, I felt fine. But these changes. Good grief. What in the world will happen to our quaint, little Sabal Palms?"

"Perhaps we should wait until after the meeting today. It might not be so bad. Let's just wait and see," Elaine said.

"Elaine, you are always so levelheaded. How do you do that?"

Elaine shrugged her shoulders. "Guess I leave it all to God. Whatever is supposed to happen will. You know that."

"Still, it's hard. I mean, I just want to do something to make it go the way *I* want it to go," Bonnie insisted.

"I know, Bonnie. It is hard to sit and let God do what He planned all along. And, speaking of doing something, how was your blood sugar today? You're several days into this new lifestyle."

"It was 101 today. Not too bad. I ate a late snack after dinner. Guess I shouldn't have done that."

"You will figure it all out. Just takes time." Elaine patted Bella on the head and picked up her keys. "Okay, Bella, you stay here. We will see you later."

Driving to Mary's house only took a few minutes, but in that short time span, Elaine noticed another realtor car pulled up to a house along the route. "Look." She pointed. "Another one."

Bonnie shook her head. "Sign of the times. *Another* one bites the dust."

Bonnie and Elaine arrived at Mary's promptly at 8:30 and found Mary on the porch waiting for their arrival. "Hey, girls. Coffee is ready."

Adriana parked behind Elaine's car, and the women soon found an array of healthy breakfast options set on Mary's kitchen table.

"Well, will you look at all these sweets!' Adriana gasped. "Is that quiche?"

"Crustless. Wait till you taste them all," Mary said. "Of course, no worries, all healthy. No sugar and no wheat flour."

Bonnie's eyes bulged. "It is wonderful! So many delicious-looking treats! You've already got this new cooking thing down!"

Mary handed Elaine a plate. "Do you think this Trent Fortune fellow will have some pictures or sketches of what he is proposing?"

Elaine nodded. "I hope so. It will make it easier for the people in town to understand what he is thinking of doing if we can see some examples."

Bonnie's mouth was full of a cinnamon roll made with almond and coconut flour, and all she could do was nod and mumble, "Uh huh," as the women chattered.

A grin spread across Adriana's face. "Whatever he is planning, I just hope it involves shopping."

Bonnie frowned and swallowed the roll. "Oh, poppycock! Shopping. Whatever he is thinking or going to say, let's hope it won't change Sabal Palms."

"New development projects usually do change a town," Mary said.

"Well, then," Bonnie huffed, "if it is going to change Sabal Palms, I hope there are enough of us likeminded people to put a stop to it."

Mary frowned. "But what if he has already purchased all the property he needs?"

"Baloney!" Bonnie snapped. "There must be something that can be done. The people of Sabal Palms must be able to have some say-so in all of this. We should try to stop this guy. Elaine, do you know anything about building permits or town restrictions?"

"I still say, build a mall! That would be amazing!" Adriana's bracelets clinked with every word she uttered.

Frustration set in. Elaine didn't want to feed this fire. Her friends seemed to be falling on different sides of this development idea, and she did not want to be in the middle. "Maybe we should wait to see what Trent says. We might all be surprised and pleased."

"Optimist!" Mary huffed.

***

The crowd outside the town hall building was too large to fit in the single meeting room in the old building. The meeting moved from the town hall building to the town hall annex just off the rear courtyard filled with blooming gardenias, jasmine, and oleanders. Elaine and her friends found seats near the front. Elaine nodded and waved to Carlos and Juan. She noticed Ramon and his wife Maria sitting with Mary's neighbor, George. Elizabeth Randolph, Myrtle Witherspoon, and Gladys from the grocery store sat near the back of the room. Martha Lewis wheeled up to the front of the meeting beside Elaine. There were several faces Elaine knew, and everyone smiled and waved to each other as they settled in for the meeting. Anyone who lived in Sabal Palms for any length of time knew each other.

Bonnie nudged Elaine and pointed. "Look, on that stand, there *are* sketches."

Elaine studied the first drawing on the easel but could not discern the meaning. It looked very green—large swatches of green behind established homes in a neighborhood. "What is it? Extension of the wildlife refuge?"

"That would be marvelous! But who knows?" Mary shrugged her shoulders and turned to Adriana, who was ogling Trent Fortune on the small stage in front of the room.

Bonnie rolled her eyes and nudged Elaine. "Will you look at her? Seriously. She won't care what he says."

Elaine laughed. "Let's give her the benefit of the doubt."

"You can. I know that look!" Mary put her finger just under her lower lip and said, "She might even have a little drool right about—"

"Oh, Mary! Honestly!"

Bonnie overheard the conversation and wasted no time chiming in. "Yep, she is like a heat-seeking missile."

"You two! Seriously?"

At that moment, Richard Townsend, the mayor of Sabal Palms, stepped onto the small stage and said a few words to Trent Fortune. Richard turned to the audience and began. "Ladies and gentlemen, fellow citizens of Sabal Palms, thank you all for coming this morning. It is my distinct pleasure to introduce Trent Fortune to you. Mr. Fortune represents Evergreen Recreation and Conservation Industries. He will present a proposal for the town of Sabal Palms. Now, I know after Jada, we have all been struggling to get back on our feet financially, individually and as a town. We all suffered through some very tough times. Mr. Fortune has a proposal that can help us get over the hump and generate revenue for some years to come. He has talked with me about his ideas, and they are sound."

At this point, Bonnie nudged Elaine and then Mary and whispered, "Here it comes."

"Mr. Fortune, I will hand these fine folks to you now."

Richard Townsend stepped down and left the small stage to Trent Fortune, who sped into the nuts and bolts of his financial assessment of Sabal Palms after Jada. Jada took a toll; and the town and the community, in general, were in a financial upheaval. Then Trent approached the first sketch and said, "And this is why Evergreen Recreation and Conservation Industries purchased several acres along the specific wildlife and ranch properties along the back side of Sabal Palms. As you can see, these green areas are the properties I already own. There are some gray areas here, and here, several here, and over here that I will be asking to buy."

Myrtle Witherspoon raised her hand and asked, "What does that mean? Asking to buy?"

"They are privately owned properties, and they have not been listed to sell—yet. I plan to approach each owner with a more-than-fair offer for the properties I would like to purchase."

"Are there homes on those properties?" Myrtle asked.

"Yes, but I am not asking to purchase all of the homes. For some of the properties with extended backyards, I am interested in purchasing only the sections of the back part of the yards—here and here and over here."

Myrtle continued, "I see. I think my home is along the left side there, on Amberjack Lane, and, well, I am turning it into a bed and breakfast. I'm not planning on selling."

The audience gasped. Heads turned as the crowd whispered to each other. This was big news in Sabal Palms. A bed and breakfast would bring tourists to stay in the town rather than on the island. Tourists would bring money but also change to the small town.

"This would, in no way, bother your home, Mrs . . . ."

"Witherspoon."

"Mrs. Witherspoon. Your bed and breakfast would be safe."

Mary leaned over to Elaine and muttered, "She probably doesn't even have her permit yet from the town."

Juan Rodriguez raised his hand in the back of the room.

"Yes, you with your hand raised in the back."

"Sir, this looks like a lot of land. What is the property being used for?"

"I am asking for a permit to build and establish a golf course."

The room fell silent.

Chapter Four

Of course, the shock did not wear off throughout the entire meeting. The citizens of Sabal Palms grilled Trent Fortune with a slate of questions that bordered on an interrogation. Trent Fortune calmly answered the onslaught and then displayed four additional sketches and color prints of his proposal. The illustrations elaborately detailed a clubhouse, a restaurant, and even a small inn for those who wanted "Stay and Play" packages that included rounds of golf, tours of Sabal Palms, a ferry ride to the island, and days on the beaches near Sabal Palms. Elaine, Mary, Bonnie, and Adriana were as amazed and bewildered by these ideas as everyone else in the meeting. Beaches near Sabal Palms could mean the beach in front of Bonnie and Elaine's cottages would be invaded by tourists.

Too befuddled to go to their own homes, the four women gathered once again on Mary's large, Southern porch. Amongst the blooming hibiscus, ferns, and swaying palms, the women ate salad topped with Parmesan cheese and grilled shrimp and drank tea and lemonade.

"What in the world is happening to our sweet, little Sabal Palms?" Adriana asked.

"*You* wanted this change!" Mary blurted.

"I wanted a mall! Not a silly, old golf course!"

"Girls, let's take a moment and think about this. Is there any benefit to bringing this golf course here?" Elaine asked.

"The town needs the money," Bonnie said. "But is it going to be worth it?"

Adriana sighed, deep in thought. "Wait, it could be worse, you know?"

Mary rolled her eyes. "How?"

"It could have been high-rise condominiums, like we talked about," Adriana said.

"That is a good point," Elaine agreed. "At least, a golf course leaves the property more natural—or even better."

Puzzled, Bonnie asked, "What do you mean?"

"It will be maintained. There will be groundskeepers, mowers, gardens, ponds, you know. You've seen golf courses on TV. They are pretty places. And after all, his company is Evergreen Recreation and Conservation Industries. That sounds like they are serious about keeping the grounds and the surrounding areas beautiful."

"Might be better for the animal habitats in the area," Mary commented. Adriana, Bonnie, and Elaine nodded and continued eating.

Bonnie's brow furrowed. "But did you hear what he said about the tourist packages including beaches near Sabal Palms?"

As much as Elaine tried not to worry, she could not deny she was worried about that comment from Trent Fortune. "Yes, I heard that. And yes, it is a concern."

"Well, what are we gonna do?" Bonnie inquired.

Before Elaine could comment, Adriana exclaimed, "And Myrtle Witherspoon! Seriously? A bed and breakfast? In Sabal Palms? What is she thinking? I never!"

Mary took up the salad dishes and huffed. "Well, I'm bamboozled by all of these changes! The development of a golf course with an inn, a bed and breakfast, a restaurant, and tour packages—and Pastor Sam leaving the church. It just won't be the same, cozy Sabal Palms."

Elaine glanced at her watch. "Nearly two o'clock. Goodness! We haven't finished planning the party for Billy. He will be here day after tomorrow."

"That's right," Bonnie agreed. "Mary, can you get some paper, so we can finalize the menu and go the grocery store? Elaine, you *are* taking us to the grocery store before we go home, right?"

Elaine nodded.

Twenty minutes later, the menu was planned, and the impromptu guest list was completed. Each had their designated tasks.

"Elaine," Mary said, "don't you think we should ask Mayor Townsend?"

"Good idea. And don't forget about asking Pastor Sam," Bonnie added.

Mary agreed. "We will have an opportunity to ask both the mayor and Pastor Sam about what is happening."

"Now, Mary." Elaine frowned.

"Well, they can tell us," Mary said.

Elaine knew that curiosity was getting the best of Bonnie, who added, "I agree. We can each casually ask them a question or two during the party."

"Promise you will all be polite," Elaine insisted. "We don't want to upset either of them We might need the mayor to help us in the future."

The women agreed.

***

The day of Billy Wrangle's welcome-back party had come. Elaine, Mary, and Adriana arrived early at Bonnie's to help prepare. They began by setting up the extra chairs and tables on the deck.

"Elaine, have you seen Billy yet?" Mary asked.

"No, he was getting settled in his rental cottage. When I talked to him yesterday on the phone, he sounded pretty excited about the party."

Mary continued, "Wonder what he will think of all these changes in Sabal Palms?"

"No idea. I'm sure he heard some of the news in town. He told me he was going to the grocery store this morning to stock up," Elaine replied.

Bonnie asserted, "Uh huh! If he was within five feet of Gladys, he will already know everything by now."

Gladys had worked at the Coastal Grocery store for over twenty years, and she told everyone she believed spreading local news was part of her civic responsibility. She often said, "Don't want folks to be caught off-guard. I want *everyone* to be prepared for what is happening in our community. We all need to know *exactly* what is going on and who is involved."

Elaine thought about what Bonnie said and replied, "Maybe Gladys talked with him. She was at the meeting. If he hasn't heard by now, he will certainly be informed after the party tonight."

Bonnie appeared outside with a box full of flameless candles. "Do you mind setting these out on the tables?"

Adriana took the box. "Splendid idea!"

"And, Elaine, I know it is a little early, but would you mind lighting the tiki torches?"

"Sure. Just take me a minute."

The soft lighting of the flameless candles, the string of twinkle lights, and the flickering light of the tiki torches set the stage for a wonderful gathering of friends, who would mingle, eat, and watch the bright orange sunset.

Pastor Sam and his wife, along with the mayor, arrived before the other guests. Within a few minutes, more cars pulled into the driveway. The guests parked along the road and in Bonnie's yard. It was going to be quite an event, and the tongues of Sabal Palms no doubt would be wagging tomorrow.

Billy was among the last to arrive. Applause broke out when he walked up the steps, dressed in his typical cowboy boots, jeans, Western shirt, and cowboy hat. Shouts of "Welcome back, Billy" filled the air.

Adriana was bouncing back and forth between the mayor and Billy.

Mary nudged Elaine. "There she goes. The social butterfly."

Bonnie laughed.

Elaine could not detect what Adriana was saying. Adriana leaned toward the mayor several times and talked lowly.

Mary rolled her eyes. "Who knows what she is up to."

"Probably fishing for information," Elaine said. "I'm going to visit with Billy for a few minutes, and then we should help Bonnie get the food out for the buffet. The guests will want to eat."

Mary nodded.

Billy hugged Elaine. "Good to see you, Elaine."

"You, too." She smiled.

"I know we can't talk specifics tonight, but tomorrow, we should set up our work schedule for the time I'm in town. I have a few ideas and I need your help."

"Sounds good. Want to come by tomorrow afternoon? Say about three or four?"

"Perfect."

Elaine and Billy managed to keep her identity a secret. The local people knew that Elaine had helped Billy with his first hit single. But no one knew they had written the lyrics for an album together and that she received royalties for each song each time it was played. The album listed the songwriters as Billy Wrangle and T. Overton. Elaine kept her finances a secret. But the little church on the seashore suddenly began receiving large donations from someone only known as "Anonymous Cheerful Giver." Pastor Sam himself had no idea it was Elaine.

Elaine sensed a commotion at the foot of the steps to Bonnie's deck. Someone had arrived, and several people flocked immediately to the steps. "What is going on?"

Mary uttered, "It's him."

Bonnie turned pale and frowned. "Money Bags."

Trent Fortune was shaking hands and greeting each of the guests.

Mayor Townsend tapped Bonnie on the shoulder. "I hope you don't mind, Bonnie, but I thought this might be a good time for Trent to mingle with the community."

Bonnie, caught completely off-guard, smiled. "Of course."

Adriana abruptly left the conversation with Pastor Sam and made a beeline to Trent.

Mary elbowed Elaine. "There she goes, like a moth to a flame."

Adriana talked in what almost seemed to be a rambling conversation.

"What is wrong with her?" Mary asked.

"Maybe she's nervous," Elaine suggested.

"Nervous, my left foot!" Mary said, rolling her eyes. "She's flirting."

Bonnie picked up a spoon and tapped a glass to get the attention of the guests. "Good evening, friends from our beautiful Sabal Palms community. Glad you could all make it tonight. As you know, our favorite singer is back in town. Welcome back, Billy."

Once again, the partygoers applauded Billy, who tipped his cowboy hat to the crowd.

"Now, please help yourselves to the buffet. And eat all you want because Bonnie, Elaine, Adriana, and I prepared a healthy menu for tonight. Even the desserts are safe."

Smiles and loud conversation took over as the guests went through the buffet and found seats at the tables spread around the deck.

Elaine glanced across the dinner party scene. It seemed magical. The glowing tiki torches and candles and the backdrop of the burnt-orange and pink sky. The sun, appearing to be a huge, orange ball, began to sink in the sky.

Elaine knew the people from the town had become closer since Jada. She thought the community would stick together. She doubted the town's people would agree to Trent Fortune's proposal if it would be detrimental to Sabal Palms. She filled her plate from the buffet options and sat next to Billy.

"Billy, have you met that fellow over there, the one talking to Adriana?" Elaine gestured.

"No. I don't think I met him last time I was here."

"He doesn't live here."

"Oh?"

"He is a developer. Says he wants to put a golf course here along the outskirts of Sabal Palms."

"Oh, that's who that is? A woman at the grocery store—uh, Gladys, I think? Anyway, she told me all about it."

"Just curious. What is your first reaction?"

"Going on what Gladys said, she wasn't too sure he was on the up-and-up. She said since he wasn't from here, she didn't trust him. She also said he put on quite a show at the town meeting the other day."

"Interesting. Yes, he did a nice presentation. Guess nobody is sure about what all of this means for our community."

Adriana left Trent and brought her plate of food to the table, where Elaine and Billy were seated. "Mind if I join you?" she asked. "Hello, Billy," She nodded in his direction. "So good to see you back in Sabal Palms."

"Good to be back, Adriana."

Thankfully, Adriana made small talk and did not immediately zing Billy with a slew of questions. But Elaine knew the questions would be sprouting soon from Adriana. She wanted to rescue Billy from a forthcoming inquisition. "Adriana, did you hear anything else from Trent about his plans?"

"No. His lips were sealed tighter than a double-zip sandwich bag. Not a peep. And Mary asked him outright if his plans were proceeding. He just changed the subject. I felt that he was avoiding it altogether. He is charming, though."

Billy laughed. "Hmmm, Adriana, are you interested? I mean, in Trent?"

Adriana waved her hand dismissively in the air. "Oh, for heaven's sakes, no. Antony is looking down at me, and he wouldn't have it." Adriana quickly made the sign of the cross on her chest between taking bites of grilled shrimp.

Billy laughed. "Had to ask. I'm always looking for material for love songs."

Adriana giggled.

At that moment, Bonnie joined the group and squeezed in close to Adriana at the table.

"Goodness," Adriana remarked. "Are you okay?"

"Heavens, yes, but dear, are you?" Bonnie asked.

Shocked, Adriana turned to Bonnie. "What are you talking about?"

"Your backyard. I heard Trent wants to buy part of your backyard."

Adriana dropped her fork onto her salad. "What? Are you sure?"

"Yes. Pastor Sam asked him generally about the other properties he wanted to buy, and he listed off several street addresses, including yours."

"No! But he can't. I won't sell it."

"Maybe I'm mistaken. But I thought he said your street. He said some of the properties along Dolphin Lane."

Adriana covered her plate with her napkin. "I think I've lost my appetite. Did he say anything else to Pastor Sam?"

"Just that he wanted to chop off about half of the backyards on those specific properties."

"But that's my pool and my pool house," Adriana protested.

Elaine was confused about how to react. She wanted to calm Adriana down, but she also wanted to help protect her. "Adriana, why don't we meet with him? We could set up an appointment in an office or at the coffee shop and see what he has to say. This isn't the right time or place to have this kind of discussion. We will find out the specifics from him in a proper meeting."

Adriana sighed, "Okay. He gave me his card with his number. I thought he might want to get together for coffee or dinner or something. Now I know why. He wants to finagle my property into his golf course."

Chapter Five

Elaine, Bonnie, and Bella went for their early morning walk. The sand warmed up as they walked along the wet strip near the water. Occasionally, the warm, foamy tide crept up and covered their feet and flip-flops. Bella scampered cheerfully along, chasing the birds and splashing into the silky water near the edge. Nose to the ground, Bella followed the crabs back into their holes and barked at each one.

"Guess we'd better get dressed for the meeting with Trent," Bonnie said.

"Bella, come on, girl. Let's go back home. We need to get ready." Bella ran to Elaine.

Elaine continued, "Maybe we'll find out that this Trent fellow is not looking to buy Adriana's backyard after all. But if he is, can you imagine?"

Bonnie shrugged her shoulders. "She would lose her pool and her pool house if she sold that part of her yard. It is such a nice, oversized backyard, and it would be down to nothing. She'd probably have to settle for a hot tub! And just think, she would have golf balls flying into her yard or even hitting her house!"

Elaine worried about this developer and his ideas all night. At the end of the welcome-back party the night before, Trent Fortune had agreed to meet with the ladies this morning in the town hall conference room.

"Bonnie, at least he'll meet with us. You know Adriana doesn't have to sell. She can just tell him no."

Bonnie stopped walking for a moment and turned to Elaine. "Here is my concern about Trent's interest in Dolphin Lane. If her neighbors are agreeable—or worse, greedy—they will pressure her to sell. It could get ugly. Oh, for crying out loud! Everything just feels so cattywampus!"

"Let's pray things will work out. In the end, we will all be following God's plans anyway," Elaine reminded her.

"How you do that, I don't know. *I* want to be in charge!" Bonnie laughed.

"Yes, but we aren't. Okay, can you be ready and come over in about thirty minutes? Mary will want us on time for coffee before we head to the meeting."

Bonnie laughed. "With four women sitting across from him, maybe Trent will come to his senses. Or maybe, there is always the possibility that we might drive him out of his mind."

Elaine laughed.

Bonnie walked up the steps to her beach cottage, and Elaine and Bella continued their journey home. "See you in a few minutes," Bonnie said from her door.

"Okay."

Elaine didn't have true business attire, since she hadn't worked in years. She picked out something that might do. She realized the capris and Hawaiian-print top weren't exactly professional-looking clothing. But the capris were ankle-length, and her shoes were the dressy sandals she wore to church. She added a small shell bracelet and tiny pearl earrings. "This is the best I have," she said, looking in the mirror.

Bonnie arrived at Elaine's top step just as Elaine opened the door to watch for her. "Good. You're here. Let's go."

She closed her front door and clicked her car remote to unlock the vehicle.

The drive was short, but for the first time in a while, there were no new realtor signs in the yards. There were, however, several caravans of realtors and buyers lined up along the way.

"There they are," Bonnie grumbled. "The invaders of Sabal Palms."

"Bonnie, what if they are all perfectly fine people, and they like Sabal Palms just the way it is? Or bring improvements?"

"Horsefeathers! Sabal Palms is perfect just the way it is right now! I like it exactly like this—picturesque." She gestured at Mary's older neighborhood.

Elaine parked the car in Mary's driveway, and Adriana pulled in right behind her.

Adriana stepped out of her sportscar in a tizzy. With dark, designer sunglasses on and jewelry blinging from her arms, neck, and ears, she said, "For heaven's sakes. I can't believe all of this is happening in our little town. If Antony was here, God rest his soul"—she made the sign of the cross on her chest—"he would know what to do. Antony, you should be here," she said, pointing her finger to the sky.

Elaine shook her head. "Adriana, we will figure this out."

The three walked to Mary's porch as Mary opened her screened door. "Good morning, ladies. Coffee and sweets are in the kitchen— healthy sweets, of course."

Elaine looked at the table and smiled. "As usual, Mary, you have outdone yourself." There were several options, and each one looked delicious.

"Adriana, what are you going to say to Trent about your property?" Bonnie asked.

"I don't even know where to begin. I don't. I thought about it all night." She took off her sunglasses and added, "Just look! Look at these *bags* under my eyes! Have you ever seen anything like these? They're not even bags; they're cargo *trunks*! I have trunks under my eyes! I got no sleep whatsoever."

Mary looked closely at Adriana's eyes and, as usual, lacking any verbal control, announced, "You'd have to weigh those bad boys at the airport to be sure they'd fit in the overhead compartment."

"Mary!" Elaine exclaimed.

"Sorry, Adriana. I don't think I've ever seen your eyes like that."

Adriana shook her head. "I know. I know. What can I do? They are positively—"

"Ugly?" Mary blurted.

"Mary! I call un-sportsman-like conduct!" Bonnie yelled.

"Girls, all of this talk of land development, buying up property, and a golf course complex has us all unnerved. Mary, I'm sure you didn't mean that," Elaine said.

"Oh, it's okay. She's right. I think these things," she said, pointing to her eyes, "are atrocious! Ice. That's what I need. Mary, do you have a dishcloth?"

Mary hopped up from her chair and retrieved a soft cloth and ice cubes. "Here you go. I'm sorry, Adriana, really. I know your eyes are beautiful. This should do the trick."

Adriana held the cloth to her eyes as she nibbled on a sweet roll and drank a cup of coffee.

"Now, back to the discussion. Adriana, what do you want to say to Trent?"

"I'm not sure. What do you think is the best strategy, Elaine?"

"If it was my property, I would want to be sure he wanted to buy it. I mean, find out if your property is actually on his list of properties to buy. And your neighbors on either side of your home. Does he want those as well?"

Adriana lowered the cloth from her eyes and asked, "Why?"

Bonnie said, "I don't know. Could be trouble."

"They could try to pressure you to sell if they want to sell—you know, bully you," Mary said.

"Wait, are you saying not only would I have to battle with Trent but also my neighbors?"

"Maybe not," Elaine said calmly. "If Trent doesn't want their properties, it would be easier to say no to him. Or if your neighbors all refused to sell. You could unite with your neighbors and agree not to sell. But in the end, no matter what, you should have the right to refuse to sell your own land."

Adriana nodded. "I certainly hope so."

Elaine thought for a moment and added, "We don't know if he wants your property and what types of permits will be required for this project. There are several questions we need to ask."

After dabbing the cloth with ice cubes on her eyes for several minutes, Adriana asked, "Should we be going?"

Mary glanced at the clock and said, "We have a little time." She picked up the coffeepot. "Anyone want a second cup?"

"Sure, I can use another," Adriana said.

Elaine agreed. "Me, too."

Holding up her cup, Bonnie added, "Let's all have more."

Mary topped off each of the cups of coffee and took another sweet roll. At that moment, her doorbell rang. "For Pete's sakes. Who is that? I'm not expecting anyone else."

Like baby ducks waddling after their mother, Adriana, Elaine, and Bonnie followed Mary to the front door.

Mary slowly opened the door and peeked through. She didn't seem to recognize the person on her porch.

"Mary! So good to see you. It's me."

Mary looked perplexed and didn't say a word.

"Your cousin, Kathy."

"For heaven's sakes! Kathy! I haven't seen you in—"

"Fifteen years," Kathy said.

"Fifteen years! Has it been that long?"

"Yes. Remember back when Charles went to work in Washington State? We haven't traveled much since then because we were so far out west."

"Well, come in. Would you like some coffee? And where are my manners? This is Adriana, Bonnie, and Elaine."

"Nice to meet you all."

The women returned to the kitchen, and Mary served Kathy a cup of coffee. "I must say, I am so shocked to see you. My goodness. All the way from the West Coast to the southern tip of Texas! Quite a journey!"

"Yes, it was a very long drive."

"You drove?"

"Yes. We wanted to have plenty of time to scout around the area. We might be relocating here."

The other three women's eyes rolled back and forth at each other. Elaine wondered if this was another person looking for a good deal on the rebuilt properties.

Kathy continued, "And my goodness, did we see some sights along the way! The first time I ever went to the Grand Canyon. Arizona, Utah, New Mexico—we saw so many new and exciting places! And who knew Texas was such a big state? We've been in Texas for two days and just got down to your neck of the woods late last night."

Elaine feared Kathy might have plenty more stories to tell the group, and they needed to leave Mary's house soon. She tilted her head toward the clock, and Bonnie picked up on the nonverbal signal.

Looking directly at Kathy and smiling, Bonnie said, "Kathy, it is so nice to meet you, but I hope you understand that we were about to leave for a meeting."

Mary joined in. "Yes, dear cousin. It is great to see you again. Maybe we can get together later this afternoon? Say, after lunch?"

Kathy replied, "I would love to, but Charles and I have a meeting at the church."

"Oh? What church?" Mary quizzed.

"The little one on the seashore."

"But why are you going there?" Mary continued.

"Charles is applying for the pastor position there."

"Oh, I see," Mary said. "That is interesting. I would love to visit more about that later. Maybe after your meeting at the church?"

"Sure, that would be terrific. Maybe this evening? Sorry if I held you ladies up from your appointment."

"No, it's okay. We will get there in plenty of time," Elaine said.

Kathy left, and the others followed out the front door.

Elaine asked the group, "Should we go in one car as usual?"

"Yes, I think so," Adriana said. "My car only holds two."

"Let's go in Elaine's car," Bonnie volunteered.

Adriana moved her car out of the way. The four women got in Elaine's car and buckled up.

Elaine knew Bonnie would not be able to contain herself. She was right. Bonnie blurted out right away. "Mary, tell us all about your cousin, Kathy."

"Now, *there* is a story!" Mary chuckled.

"Tell us!" Bonnie insisted.

"It is a very long story. Not sure I want to get into all of that right now. I am focused on this Trent fellow and what we are going to say to him," Mary said. "But I will tell you all about her later. She is an interesting character."

"Perhaps we should refocus," Elaine agreed.

Mary nodded. "Yes, that surprise visit threw me for a loop. I have to get my brain back on task."

In a panic, Adriana waved her arms in the crowded car and exclaimed, "You girls are scaring me! We have to look like we think we might know what we are talking about."

"But we don't," Mary said.

"Come on now, ladies. Remember, we decided earlier to ask Trent Fortune if Adriana's property is one of the properties he is interested in buying and see the status of his plan. Do Adriana's neighbors want to sell? Does he have permits? How is everyone else in the community reacting? You know, those kind of questions."

"No one can accuse you of slippage! You remembered all the details." Mary chuckled.

Entering the parking lot, Elaine laughed. "Well, here we are. Are we ready?"

"Wait! Wait!" Adriana insisted.

"For what?" Bonnie asked.

"I need to look in the mirror. Are they gone?"

"Who?" Bonnie asked.

"The bags under my eyes?"

"Oh, malarkey! Stop lollygagging, and let's get in there!" Mary insisted.

"Your eyes look fine," Elaine reassured her.

***

The receptionist took the four women to the conference room. "Mr. Fortune phoned he was running late, but he is on his way. He is crossing the causeway as we speak."

"Thank you," Elaine said.

Elaine, Mary, Bonnie, and Adriana took seats around the table and waited.

"Wonder what he is up to," Adriana said.

"Shhh!" Mary said and pointed to the large conference call microphone on the table.

"What?" Adriana asked, shrugging her shoulders and throwing her hands in the air.

Mary pointed again and whispered, "They're listening."

"Who?" Bonnie asked.

"I don't know, but you never know if one of these machines is on or not," Mary said.

"Horsefeathers!" Bonnie said.

The door opened. Elaine turned to see Trent Fortune, with his twinkling eyes; slicked-back hair; crisp, white shirt; and khaki pants, walking in bigger than life. *His persona fills up the whole room*, she thought.

"Ladies, good to see you again. That was quite the dinner party last night, Bonnie."

"Thank you."

"And Billy Wrangle. I didn't see that coming. Here in little Sabal Palms. It's nice to know, as an investor, that the town is drawing some very talented people to the area. Now, I'll bet I know what brings you in today. I am guessing it is to ask me questions about the development?"

Bonnie nudged Adriana, who was in a trance with her eyes locked on Trent.

"Oh, yes," Adriana said. "That is exactly why we are here. You see, I am wondering about the properties you said you are interested in buying."

"I see. And are you an owner of a home in Sabal Palms?"

"Yes. I live on Dolphin Street."

"Yes, I think there are some properties there. I am continuing to study that particular area. In fact, I was just out setting up some drone flyovers of that area to assess what portions we would need for the golf course."

Bonnie rolled her eyes.

Mary grumbled, "Drones."

"Oh, I take it you don't care for the drone flyovers? Shouldn't be too many, just over the neighborhood that you mentioned in the Dolphin, Amberjack and Blue Marlin area. Oh, and also along Sabal Palms Beach. I might be flying my plane over that way to scout the beach from the air. We're looking there to develop a tourist area for those who would book a stay-and-play package."

Elaine sat up and leaned toward Trent across the table. "Tourist area? On the beach?"

"Yes. We can shuttle the tourists over there and drop them off for a beach trip. We plan to have a beachside café, picnic tables, covered areas, and lounge chairs with umbrellas set out all along the beach."

Elaine's heart sank. Her quiet, peaceful beach would be run over by a parade of interlopers. It would never be the same. Strange people would be lurking about in front of her house and between her cottage and Bonnie's cottage. The pristine sand would be littered. No doubt, the intertidal anthropoids, waterfowl, and sea creatures would be disturbed.

Elaine got up her courage and asked, "How far along are you in your planning? Do you have the necessary permits and such? And is zoning an issue?"

Trent, somewhat stunned, leaned back in his chair. "We're working on all of those concerns and should have our proposals ready soon. Trust me, the details are in the works." Turning to Adriana, he said, "What is your exact address, Adriana?"

"Oh, uh, fifty-five Dolphin Lane."

"You must live next door to Thomas Williams?"

"Yes, he is to the left of my property."

"Quite the golfer. Did you know that?"

"I had no idea."

"Yes. He is the reason I'm here."

Shocked, Adriana asked, "What do you mean?"

"I met him playing golf in Florida. We played a couple of rounds and he told me all about Sabal Palms. He knew I was a developer and specialized in communities like yours. He invited me down to see the town. And now, here we are, putting together a proposal for the recreational permits and zoning requirements. He is very interested in selling his property."

Adriana's face was pale.

"Now, I'm sorry to cut this meeting short, but I worked this meeting in between a couple of other things. I have a phone conference in about sixty-seconds."

At that moment, the speaker buzzed.

"Oh, oh, of course." Elaine stood up, as did the other three women, sensing they had been dismissed. With mouths gaping open, the other women followed her out the conference room door.

Halfway down the hallway, Elaine realized her keys were on the conference room table. "Go ahead, girls. I'll sneak back in there and grab my keys."

The conference door remained slightly cracked open, and Elaine crept in to retrieve her keys. Trent Fortune was in the middle of his phone conference on the speaker phone. Elaine pointed to her keys and walked over and picked them up.

Trent nodded.

Walking back out the door, she overheard Trent say, "Yes. Oh, the church doesn't even have a pastor right now, so it should be easier than we thought. No, it won't be a problem."

Elaine's stomach was in knots. Jada was a storm of nature. This coming storm was worse. This storm was evil. There may be no way to take cover.

Chapter Six

The women sat in complete silence in the car on the way back to Mary's house. Elaine didn't want to tell the others what she had overheard. She wanted to find out more about Trent and what he intended to do with the church before she said anything. Maybe what she'd overheard wasn't as bad as she feared.

It was difficult to know who was more upset about the meeting. Thinking of the comments she'd overheard Trent saying on the phone upset her, even though she wasn't sure of the meaning. She knew Bonnie would also worry that their beautiful beach would be disturbed and their lives would be chaos with streams of tourists. Elaine could sense Adriana was upset about her neighbor, Thomas Williams, being the one responsible for getting this project started in the first place and that he was willing to sell out.

Mary broke the silence. "I feel helpless about the developments. I wonder what this new development might do the wildlife. I'm shocked my cousin, Kathy, whom I haven't seen in fifteen years, suddenly appeared at my front door. This all feels so crazy. Are we on another planet?"

"More like the twilight zone," Bonnie snapped.

"It is very upsetting. All of it," Elaine agreed.

Elaine parked the car in the drive of Mary's house. The four women, who seemed to be in a zombie-like state, walked to the porch without speaking.

"Lunch? I have healthy chicken salad, green salad, and low-carb bread," Mary said.

Elaine smiled at the invitation. "Thank you, Mary. That sounds delicious."

"I'm in," Bonnie said.

"Okay. I could eat something," Adriana agreed.

"Come inside. It will just take me a minute to put it all out."

Less talkative than usual, the women gathered in the breakfast nook of Mary's spacious kitchen to eat their lunch and sip tea. The few comments that were made concerned the tasty chicken salad and the homemade bread.

In an effort to brighten the mood, Mary asked, "Would you like to have dessert on the porch? I have some fresh blueberries and cream."

"That sounds lovely," Adriana said softly.

The summer heat was held in check by a partly cloudy sky, slight sea breeze, and whirring ceiling fans all along the expansive front porch.

"There's just no place like Sabal Palms." Elaine sighed.

"I agree. And, honey, let me tell you, I have been places," Adriana said, gesturing toward the sky. "I have flown all over the world and visited so many places when dear Antony"—she paused to cross herself—"was alive." Surprisingly, Adriana cut her extensive reiteration of her travels short. It was clear the meeting had disturbed her.

The women enjoyed every morsel of their dessert, and the breeze brought comfort and calming. The peace was soon disturbed by the most irritating noise from out of nowhere.

"What? What is that?" Bonnie said.

"Huh?" Mary asked.

"Oh no. Look!" Adriana pointed to a large drone heading their way.

"It's already started. Next will be bulldozers, trucks, and construction crews!" Mary huffed.

"There will be construction trash flying all over, men yelling, metal outhouses placed all along the roads and beach, and the loud backup beeping on all of the equipment! It will be a disaster!" Bonnie screeched.

"Elaine," Adriana said, "you are the most strategic and organized person in our group. What can we do?"

"I suggest we educate ourselves."

Surprised, Mary asked, "Huh? About what?"

"Everything having to do with this project. Trent must make it all public. The whole community should be provided with all the details. We need to find out the details and the process before he tells the community, so we can be armed with questions. Maybe we pull Gladys into the conversation."

Bonnie laughed. "Have you lost your mind? Gladys will tell everyone . . . Oh, wait, Gladys *will* tell everyone!"

They all laughed.

Elaine nodded. "Now you see. Here's what we can do. Study his plans. Study the town ordinances, the county permits—everything we can possibly find. Then we'll get Gladys in on it to let her know what is happening. She can help us to organize."

Mary's eyes opened wide as saucers. "Organize?"

"Yes. It is up to the citizens of our community to decide if this is a good move or not—good for the community and for every single property owner."

Adriana hung on Elaine's every word. "And then? What then, Elaine?"

"I haven't gotten that far." She hesitated. "But we will figure it out. I know we can."

Bonnie chuckled. "Always the optimist."

"In the meantime, I have a meeting with Billy in about an hour. But tonight, I will do some research. Can we meet again tomorrow morning?"

Adrian spoke up. "Yes. Want to come to my place? I will get my laptop and printer ready. I have reams of copy paper and lots of office supplies. Antony overstocked the office years ago. Even have extra binders. If we need to make copies of your findings, I can make copies, and we will read through things together."

"Perfect. I will bring over a list of articles for us to look over. If we think they will help our cause, we'll print and study each one. Then we will organize our findings. And now, ladies, I have a meeting in a while with Billy. Bonnie, are you ready to get back to the beach?"

"I am."

***

Elaine's thoughts raced back and forth between the meeting with Billy and the research yet ahead of her today to get to the bottom of Trent Fortune's plans. Billy was due in ten minutes. She retrieved her paper tablet and pens and waited on her deck. Right on time, Billy's truck drove into her drive.

Billy opened the truck door, grabbed his guitar, and tipped his hat. "Hello, Elaine."

"Hi. Come on up. I made some fresh lemonade. I'll bring it out if you want to sit outside."

"You know I do. Can't see this view in Nashville." He gestured toward the beach.

Elaine returned with two large glasses of lemonade. "Tell me about the song you are working on, and then, we should plan our schedule for the next few weeks."

Billy started talking about his song—a love song about a person who thought he might have found the love of his life. This prompted Elaine to ask, "Okay, tell me, is this song a true story? Have you found another girlfriend?"

"Not exactly. And that is what is puzzling me about the song. The melody came to me, but it is missing the lyrics. The tune—it's a longing tune. The notes are begging for a partner. At least, that's the way it feels to me. Like there is an element missing."

"And what do you suppose that element is?"

"Longing. I am longing to find this person but haven't found her yet. I am thinking maybe the album might have a similar theme. Longing for love."

"Hmmm. I will give that some thought as we work through the next weeks. Can you play any of the melody yet?"

"Yes, not sure about a chorus or what will be stressed yet in the music. But here goes."

Billy played the notes to a beautiful, yet eager-sounding, song. It seemed to Elaine that it was building up to something that had not been included yet at the end.

"That's wonderful. I do hear the eagerness in the tune, and like you said, it seems to be wanting at the end. Do you mind if I record it on my phone? I can play this over and do a little research."

"Research?"

"Yes, Billy, for inspiration, I read Scripture. It will come to me. I am thinking Psalms or Song of Songs."

"Well now, those are good places to look. I will study the versus also," he agreed.

"Perfect! We will come up with just the right words for that melody."

"Yes, ma'am. We always do."

Elaine set her phone to audio record, and Billy played the melody again.

"Okay, Billy, let me get my calendar, and we can figure out our workdays."

Elaine returned to the deck. "Are you going to schedule fishing trips this month?"

"Yes, I've discovered I am a huge fan of deep-sea fishing. I met a captain last trip who said he will set aside several days for me this month."

"What is his name? Wonder if I know him."

"Interesting person. Captain Robert. He told me his whole family history and that he was named after a famous sea captain."

"Really? Who?"

"Captain Robert Stockton. Said this guy was in the Mexican-American War."

"That is quite a tale."

"Yes. And turns out, the original Captain Robert Stockton really was in that war and a famous sea captain."

"Guess you learn something every day."

Billy nodded. "Yep. Always learn new things when I visit Sabal Palms. Oh, I wanted to ask you."

"Yes?"

"What Gladys said about the land developer. You know I met him at the party at Bonnie's house. What do you think about him and about the project?"

"He was quite impressed with you. But, Billy, I am afraid it is worse than we thought."

"How?"

"He wants to develop the area in Adriana's neighborhood, including part of her backyard. He is proposing a golf course with a clubhouse, restaurant, and inn. Oh, and he is planning on tour packages to the beach in Sabal Palms and to the island."

"Oh, Elaine, I am sorry to hear this. Bringing the golf course in would mean more money for Sabal Palms. But at what expense to landowners? And to the seashore? Look at this view. I don't want this to change."

"I'm not sure he has all of his permits approved yet. He's surveying the whole area. Complete with drones flying all around neighborhoods. There is still hope we can stop it. If not, maybe we can change the specifics of his ideas for buying portions of people's properties and for including the beach."

"Ah, that's my girl! Don't give up."

"You know me well. No way we are going to stand by."

"Bonnie, Adriana, and Mary are all in on helping?"

"Yes. We're meeting again tomorrow to get started."

"That's good, Elaine. Let me know if there is anything I can do."

"Thanks, Billy. I will."

"I mean it. Anything at all. I know people who might be able to help us."

"Us?"

"Yes. I am going to buy property here in Sabal Palms soon. I want to be involved in keeping this place beautiful."

"Here? Oh, that's exciting news, Billy. I am beyond thrilled to know you will be here often."

"I figured, why keep renting? I can buy someplace to stay when I am here for extended periods of time."

"It makes sense. Now, let's look at this calendar."

Elaine and Billy planned several workdays over the next few weeks. Billy was in town for a month, but he said he would extend his stay if needed.

"Okay, Elaine. This schedule looks good. I will let you get back to your evening. See you in a couple of days."

"Thanks, Billy. And I will work on researching those Scriptures."

***

Following her evening walk with Bonnie, Elaine got right back to her research. She turned on her computer and got to work. There was much research to do before she met with Adriana, Mary, and Bonnie. She started first with the zoning ordinances and building permits for the town and county. She continued working into the night, digging up every ordinance, zoning regulation, and even the town ordinances for property and development changes to this area of the state. She would be ready for the meeting tomorrow and would walk her friends through every paragraph, every sentence, every word.

Elaine touched the power button on her computer then remembered. She had one more topic to research. She would investigate Trent Fortune.

She began with a general Google search and jotted down all the entries about Trent. There were Fortune 500 topics with his name. Television interviews. Even entries on YouTube. She noticed his Facebook page. There were newspaper articles. In fact, there were probably a hundred articles written on Trent. Why had she never heard of him before? There had to be a reason. If he was this famous, this wealthy, why hadn't she known about him?

Elaine sat in silence. Then she prayed. There was so much to sort out and sift through, it would be like finding a needle in a haystack.

"Come on, mystery man. There must be something useful in here," she whispered.

Bella sat up, then laid back on her bed, realizing Elaine was speaking to the computer and not to her.

Skimming through the newspaper articles, one title caught her eye: "Trent Fortune Remodels Church."

Was this a good thing? she wondered.

She clicked on the title. The article was from a small newspaper in the South. It was in a small town on the coast of Louisiana. She read through the article. The first sentence of the second paragraph hit her like a brick. She read it again and again. Then she read it aloud. "Fortune said his belief in New Age religion inspired him to buy out the church." She was in shock. *New Age religion? What is that? Is it a cult or something?*

Whatever it was, it wasn't good. There is only one true faith, and it began with Creation. The only true religion had been documented for over three thousand years. Nothing new about it.

In a panic, Elaine Googled New Age Religion. Her mouth dropped. She could not believe what was before her eyes. Reading through the information, she mumbled words randomly. "Cosmology, individual practices, meditation, walking on hot coals, man is God? What is this garbage?" She read through other interpretations of New Age. The articles rambled on, and she continued to say the strange findings. "This covers everything from quantum physics to crystals, and universal energy."

She was exhausted but looked up one last Bible verse before calling it a night.

"'Beloved, do not believe every spirit, but test the spirits to see whether they are from God, for many false prophets have gone out into the world'—1 John 4:1."

"Yes, false prophets," she whispered.

At two a.m., her eyes were blurry, and she couldn't stay awake any longer. She turned off the computer. Her morning beach walk with Bonnie was just a few short hours away. After the walk, Bonnie and Elaine would meet the others at Adriana's house. Tomorrow, the meeting would likely continue most of the day.

Chapter Seven

The roar of thunder woke Elaine at 5:35 a.m. The echoing was rolling from out at sea. This time of year, the storm would be heading to shore from the south. It was unexpected. The weather forecast the night before did not include even a hint of rain. But that is how it was in the summer at Sabal Palms. Without warning, thunderstorms, sometimes severe and sometimes with waterspouts, popped up now and again.

"Bella, come on, girl. You need to make a quick run outside before the storm gets here."

Bella wagged her nub of a tail and followed Elaine to the front door. In a way, Elaine was relieved that her beach walk with Bonnie would have to wait until this afternoon. She wanted to tell Bonnie what she had discovered late last night but preferred to tell it to Adriana and Mary at the same time.

Bella made a dash to the bottom of the stairs and went to the yard behind the house. In this small, green space, a grove of twenty-year old palm trees, a lone avocado tree, and a small lime tree stood. The smaller avocado and lime trees had emerged after Jada. Bella promptly did her business and scampered back up the steps.

"Good girl. Come on, let's get you an early breakfast."

Elaine waited until daylight to be sure Bonnie was up and called her. "Good morning. Looks like we will have to wait until later to get some exercise."

"Yes. Sounds good. Suppose you could swing over and pick me up to go to Adriana's house in a bit?"

"Of course. Wouldn't want you out in the elements."

"Thank you. Guess you will be here in about an hour and a half?"

"Perfect. You have your breakfast already?" Elaine did not want to worry about Bonnie having any trouble with her blood sugar during this crisis time with Trent Fortune and his development projects. She knew that stress could cause blood sugar to rise.

"Just about to make me some eggs and a bit of strawberries."

"Good. Stay healthy. Okay, I'll see you soon."

Elaine ate, dressed, and decided to use the remaining time to read more about New Age religion. She turned her computer on and scrolled through the topics. She was horrified. The more she read, the more sickened she felt. One research report stunned her to the core. The report stated that over sixty percent of Christians thought there was truth in the concepts of New Age religion.

You can meet somewhere else—not in my church on the shore, she thought.

She gathered her notes, turned her computer off, and picked up her car keys.

"Okay, Bella, I'll see you in a while. We can go for our walk later," she said, patting the pooch on the head.

Although Bonnie and Elaine lived on the same street, it was quite a bit shorter going by way of the beach on foot than by the road. In a car, it took nearly eight minutes. Elaine meandered down the road and turned into Bonnie's drive. Bonnie appeared before Elaine could honk the horn. She crept to the car, stepping around puddles. .

"Well, this rain was unexpected," Bonnie said, snapping the umbrella closed.

"It certainly was. Glad that little storm came through. The palm trees were getting thirsty!"

Bonnie nodded. "Elaine, I hope you have a game plan for us. I am getting more anxious. I mean, we don't *own* the beach in front of our cottages. I'm afraid a developer can do whatever he wants, since it's not our personal property. Trent Fortune. What a name. What a character. Flying his plane over our beach! A bunch of malarkey, if you ask me. He even said, 'Trust me.' That's a sign right there the man can't be trusted!"

Elaine thought Bonnie was a little more intense than usual. She wanted to calm her down a bit before they talked about specifics. "I found a few things that might help us. We can read through them all and discuss ideas of what to do. I think we have more time to work on our defense than we might have imagined."

"Good. That is good news."

Elaine turned into Adriana's driveway. Mary's car was already there. "Okay, looks like we are all here."

With umbrellas overhead, the two traipsed through the front yard and up the porch steps. The hanging ferns dripped water all over the steps. The door opened. "Come in, ladies, come in," Adriana motioned.

"Hello, girls," Mary said from Adriana's kitchen. "I'm warming up a coffee cake."

"Terrific day for a coffee cake," Bonnie said.

"Silly girl! *Every* day is a terrific day for a coffee cake!" Mary chuckled.

With small plates of coffee cake and cups of coffee encircling the large breakfast table in Adriana's oversized kitchen, the questions began.

Adriana asked the first question. "So, Mary, about your cousin?" She jangled her bracelets as she poured her coffee.

"My lands, she is something else. But look, she hasn't had time to visit yet. Once I can get her to bring Charles over, I will find out what is going on."

Bonnie then burst out, "Spill it, Elaine. I know you found something in those papers. Tell us what you found!"

Mary added, "Do we have legal grounds to stop this . . . this Trent fellow?"

Adriana asked, "Can he force the community to go along with this?"

Elaine replied, "There are things we can do. I found information on zoning regulations on the town of Sabal Palms Planning and Commission webpage and the Cameron County local government page."

"Really? There are things we can do?" Adriana asked.

"Yes. There are actions we can take. I have it all written down here, and we can print these pages off to read after we finish our coffee cake."

"I might get just a drop more coffee," Bonnie said, already at the coffee pot. "Anyone else?"

All heads nodded, and the ladies filled their cups.

"And I need a dab more coffee cake," Mary said.

Darting out of the room, Adriana hollered, "I'll get my laptop and turn on the printer."

"I'm already feeling better about this invasion of the developer," Bonnie said.

"Oh, that's your improved blood sugar talking." Mary laughed.

"No, I think it's the caffeine!" Bonnie quipped. "That storm this morning woke me up too early."

Elaine smiled. "You're going to want to be fully awake for what we are about to read."

Adriana read the topics and entered the articles into the search engine, and Elaine specified which pages to print. Within fifteen minutes, two cups of coffee, and more than a helping's worth of coffee cake, the ladies were ready to begin their work.

"Let's start with the Sabal Palms information first. It will be helpful for the beach and Trent's big ideas about the tourist excursions."

The women read the pages and underlined phrases and placed asterisks for the important concepts.

"Looks like this says we can have this brought before the commissioners if we wish to protest Trent's proposed changes," Adriana said.

Bonnie nodded. "Yes, and we need to have at least twenty percent of the property owners on board to petition for this hearing. Is that the way you interpret it, Elaine?"

"That is what I thought it said also, but there is more."

"Yes, there is," Mary said. "Let's see, there is the zoning commission and the commission's court. We must petition to the zoning commission, who will then take it on our behalf to the commissioner's court. And there will be a public hearing."

"And that is when we get the whole town to turn up. In fact, before that, we need to get the other property owners together to sign off that they want this report from the committee and to have the hearing," Bonnie said.

"And! Oh! Oh! Look! It also says it is not just the property itself but anything two hundred feet behind the property! I have the right to say no not just to my land but to the two hundred feet behind it! This is amazing!" Adriana clapped her hands, which sent one of her bracelets flying straight into the remaining coffee cake. "Oops! Sorry."

"No problem," Mary said lifting the bracelet out of the cake. "But it damaged the look of the cake, so I will just eat the damaged part."

"Now, ladies, we have to watch the calendar. It says the hearing must take place before the tenth day before the zoning commissioners meeting," Elaine warned. "And after that, after the hearing, the commissioners will take it up at the following zoning meeting."

Adriana smiled. "I have to say, this is really good news!"

Mary ducked down.

"What are you doing?" Adriana asked.

"I was ducking in case you were gonna launch another bracelet my way," Mary teased.

"I think the only safe thing to do is finish off the rest of the coffee cake—you know, so it won't get messed up by any other flying jewelry." Bonnie laughed.

"There's not much left. Anyone want a couple of bites?" Adriana asked.

With the coffee cake put to rest, Elaine was ready to introduce chapter two of this research. She would save the worst part about the church to the end. She anticipated that discussion might go beyond lunch and well into the afternoon.

Each of the women read through the longer documents of the Cameron County zoning regulations. Occasionally, one of the ladies would groan or say, "I didn't know that."

Twenty minutes later, the discussions began. Mary was first, which was pretty typical in conversations.

"These have a similar process to the town of Sabal Palms, but it includes an appellate process. Good grief, do we need a lawyer?"

Adriana looked shocked. "Not a fan of lawyers since I went through all the proceedings after Antony's death, God rest his soul." The habitual sign of the cross followed.

Elaine sighed. "I'm not sure we need one. But I don't think it would hurt."

"Look at all of this gobbledygook! It says, blah blah, writ, and restraining order—oh, hogwash! We are gonna need an attorney!" Mary screeched.

"For the love of Pete! How are we going to pay for *that?*" Bonnie asked.

"Well, I don't know, but we are gonna have to! Mark my words. We can't march into these meetings by ourselves. This guy has money—you know, deep pockets, very deep pockets, probably to China!" Mary turned to Elaine. "What do you think, Elaine? Should we talk to an attorney?"

"I don't think it would hurt. I'm sure we can find the money somehow, somewhere."

Elaine knew it was no use arguing with the ladies about whether or not to hire an attorney. She knew that Trent probably didn't care about these four women in the community or others who had the best interest of Sabal Palms at heart. Trent was used to rubbing elbows with the rich and famous. He would throw all kinds of money into his cause. He would do whatever it took to get this project approved.

"What should we do next, then, Elaine?" Mary asked. "Should we interview attorneys? Should we search for attorneys who represent people going against the local governments?"

A lightbulb turned on in Elaine's mind. "Wait, I have a thought."

All eyes turned to Elaine, waiting for her next nugget of wisdom.

"I think I will ask Billy. He knows plenty of attorneys and people who use attorneys. There are several Nashville singers who own property in Texas as well as Nashville. I think he can help us out. They all know attorneys, I'm sure."

"You think so?" Adriana asked.

"Won't hurt to ask," Elaine said. Then choosing her words carefully, she said, "And there is something else that happened yesterday."

Now the women's eyes were fixated on her, watching Elaine intently and waiting to hear her next words.

"You know I had to sneak back in and get my car keys off the table in the conference room?"

They nodded.

"I overheard something when I was in the conference room, and I wanted to research it before I brought it up to you all. I wanted to see what we are up against."

Still silent and looking fearful, the three women hung on every word.

Elaine continued. "You recall Trent told us he had a conference call?"

"Yes," Mary said.

"And?" Bonnie asked.

"I'm not sure what it means, but I heard him say, 'Yes. Oh, the church doesn't even have a pastor right now, so it should be easier than we thought.' Then he said something about he was sure there wouldn't be a problem."

"I knew he was a hornswoggler from the beginning!" Mary shouted. "Charlatan! Con artist!"

"Crook!" Bonnie added.

Elaine stopped the bantering. "Okay, this isn't helping."

"Sorry, Elaine," Mary said. But have you ever? Somebody wants to tear down the church for a tourist development?"

"But that's just it," Elaine said.

"What?" Mary asked.

"Spill it, Elaine," Bonnie said. "What is it?"

"I am not so sure he wants to tear it down."

"What?" Adriana asked. "Well, what on earth would he do with it?"

"I am afraid it is worse than that. I am afraid he wants to change it."

Adriana looked perplexed. "Change it to what?"

"In my research last night, I found newspaper articles, television interviews—you name it. Trent Fortune is so wealthy, it is unbelievable. And not only does he buy properties and put in resort areas, but he is also a follower of New Age religion. He had done this before. He changed a traditional church into something else."

"I don't understand," Bonnie said.

"What does that mean, anyway? New Age?" Adriana asked.

"It's this so-called 'new movement,' which has been around for a while. Now, it's pulling more Christians away from the church. In fact, it is so crazy, I couldn't figure out exactly what it is supposed to represent—except that each person defines it their own way, and they think that man is God."

"That is ridiculous!" Adriana huffed.

"Sounds like gibberish to me!" Mary grumbled.

Bonnie agreed with Mary. "Right? Absurd foolishness! But, Elaine, there *can't* be a big following of people who actually believe this garbage?"

Elaine sighed. "Sadly, one report from the Pew Research Center stated over sixty percent of Christians accept at least one of these beliefs as true."

"What?" Mary gasped.

"Horrendous!" Bonnie said.

"How can they?" Adriana asked. "Just sounds like a bunch of mealy-mouthed drivel."

"Now, the real question is, what do we do about it?" Elaine asked.

The women talked all day and, in the end, decided to meet again in the morning to talk further about the possibility of hiring an attorney and plan detailed steps for their next moves to involve the community. They would continue meeting until they figured out what the community could do to address this development project. Trent's evil intentions had to be stopped.

Chapter Eight

Frowning at the smudge on the nameplate, Trent took his handkerchief from his pocket and wiped down the gold plate. "Trent Fortune," he whispered, polishing his name on his Florida office door. He had not wanted to make the quick trip back to his Florida home, but the truth of the matter was that he needed to meet with his investors face-to face. He pushed his intercom button.

"Yes, Mr. Fortune?"

"Shirley, can you ask catering to bring in lunch for four precisely at noon? The others should be here any moment."

"Yes, sir."

Trent sat in his desk and turned his chair a bit. He never tired of the view from the penthouse office suite overlooking the south end of Miami toward the southern tip of Florida. He took pleasure telling people he could see Key Largo from his office window. In reality, following Highway US-1, it was over sixty miles. But it made for a good story. And telling good stories and half-truths was something Trent mastered many years ago. After all, he had properties in Key Largo, so he didn't mind telling a little white lie if it helped him close a deal.

The intercom buzzed.

"Yes, Shirley?"

"Mr. Franklin and Mr. Dinero are here. And Mr. Green is on his way up the elevator."

"Thank you. Escort them in, please."

The long hallway from Shirley's reception office to Trent's office was designed to impress. The views ranged from the Atlantic Ocean along one wall to lighted collectable art displays and historic pirate artifacts on shelving along the other wall. No doubt, his guests would be dazzled by Trent's surroundings.

Shirley opened the door. "Gentlemen"—she gestured to Franklin and Dinero—"please come in."

Greeting his investors, Trent said, "Hello. Franklin and Dinero. Glad you could make it on short notice." He walked over and shook the hands of his guests, whom he had habitually called by only their last names. In turn, they simply called him "Trent," and he wondered if it was some underhanded powerplay to keep him in his place. It reminded him of a demeaning way his own father said "son" to him. Same tone of voice, like Trent was always inferior.

Trent recalled how these investors first recruited him into the New Age movement. They assured him it would be much easier to strike a deal with them—and all subsequent investment deals—if he went along with their ideas about each being their own god. It was consistent with Trent's own ambitiousness and greediness. He had heard about these ideas in college. But now, the more he heard about these beliefs, the more he believed.

Trent motioned for them to each have a seat at the conference table.

Shirley buzzed once again. "Mr. Fortune, the caterer is here. Oh, and Mr. Green as well."

"Wonderful. Bring them in, please."

Green, the last investor to enter the room, shook hands with Trent and the other investors and sat at the long table. The caterer pulled the buffet cart covered with scrumptious, expensive entrees, sides, and desserts near the conference table. The presentation of each dish would easily make a cover shot for *Bon Appétit* magazine.

Shirley took her usual seat at the side of the table, ready to take notes during the meeting.

"Gentlemen. It is so good of you to come. Please, help yourselves to lunch. Feel free to serve yourselves and enjoy lunch while I explain the details of the project in Sabal Palms."

Trent opened his laptop and prepared to start the PowerPoint presentation. It was a comprehensive report, complete with financial analysis and diagrams of the potential golf course, clubhouse, restaurant, and inn. The last part of the presentation included drone shots of the beach and the little church on the seashore.

"Now, shall we get started? Continue to enjoy your lunch and don't forget the desserts."

The investors listened intently as Trent explained each screen. They asked enough questions to show their interest but not so many that would indicate skepticism about the plausibility of the project. Trent was pleased with their reactions. He wanted others to sink some money into the project, so it wouldn't have to be funded only by his assets. When he finished the golf course portion of the proposal, he changed to the first picture of the beach.

"That is one clean-looking beach. Calm water, on the bay across the Laguna Madre, nice. This looks like a real find," Green said.

Franklin nodded. "Couldn't agree more. Who knew this little piece of perfection was at the southern tip of Texas?"

Dinero put down his fork and cleared his throat. "I noticed there are a few houses there along the beach. Think that will be a problem?"

"I don't think so. I found out there are a couple of widows living along that stretch of the beach, and not far from there, another home with a Hispanic couple. I assume they will not turn down a fair price for the property. And if they turn it down, I will offer enough to persuade them. I only need to find the right price."

Franklin nodded, "Everyone has a price, right?"

Around the table, they all laughed in agreement.

Dinero continued with his questions. "And let me play devil's advocate here; what if these widows and this Hispanic couple are die-hard beach people who refuse to leave? Suppose there is no amount of money you can offer them?"

"That's doubtful. But there are other methods. I'm checking into the proper zoning, permits, and the like. If they refuse to leave, we can look at possible condemnation of the property. If that doesn't work, we'll request to take a portion of the beach for access just beyond the houses, and the tourists can walk along to the beachside park included in the proposal. We can establish a designated walkway there."

The other three nodded their heads in agreement.

Trent moved forward to the next shot of the little church. "And this is the structure I mentioned in the email."

The three investors sat up and looked closely at the picture.

"It is exactly like you described," Mr. Franklin commented.

"I like it," Mr. Dinero agreed. "Right there on the shore—lots of eternal, universal energy rising up from the sea. Wonderful."

Mr. Green smiled and nodded. "And the community—how do they feel about changing the church? Being repurposed for us?"

"I discovered, quite by mistake, from a cashier in their local grocery store, that the pastor of the church is leaving. They don't have a replacement. I think we can approach the church-hiring committee or executive committee—whatever they call it—and tell them the church needs to be remodeled. I've already made certain of that. One candidate will be interviewed by the committee in the next day or so. We will have influence. And of course, we would like to donate the funds. The structure has been there since 1925 and has been damaged several times by hurricanes."

"And again, playing devil's advocate, what if the committee doesn't go along with this remodeling proposal or hires someone else and they don't agree with repurposing for our own New Age philosophy?" Franklin asked.

Trent replied, "I have several ideas. First, as mentioned, the structure had repeated damage over the years. We call in our own inspection team. No one will know it's our team, and they will provide us with a condemnation report due to black mold, termites, structural problems, and so on."

Dinero chuckled. "I like it."

Franklin looked baffled. "Wait, I have another question about the changing of the church's mission and religion. How do we get the community to accept our beliefs? They may be against New Age."

Trent smiled and said, "Just like we did all of the others. We will go ahead with the golf course project and slowly introduce our beliefs into the community propaganda-style."

Franklin smiled. "Social media, plant a few influencers in the community, socialize to recruit the spiritually weak. It has worked well before."

"Yes, indeed," Green said. "Working all over the country as we speak."

The men all laughed.

"Are we good with the numbers? The assessment and cost-benefit ratios check out?" Trent asked.

Franklin looked through several pages of numbers once more. "Yes. It looks good. Everything checks out. Do we know when the local governments approve everything, permits and so on? If we know that, we can set up the project accounts and—"

"Oh," Green interrupted. "Sorry, hate to interrupt, but remember that development and church property project in Alabama?"

Trent said, "I do. But I don't think this small town will muster up a defense against the proposal at the town or county level. This sleepy, little place, finally recovering from Jada, will not protest. Sabal Palms is not heavily populated. No real industry there. Surely, no one lives in this little town who would organize against a company this size. We will stay one step ahead. If they do try to protest or file an injunction, our attorneys will cause their attorneys to submit huge stacks of billable hours; nobody in that town has the net worth to pay large sums of money to attorneys. I've checked out the median income of the town and the real estate value in the area. In fact, the way I see it, the town is hungry for someone to come in and pay them overpriced amounts for their properties. In the past year, since the hurricane, the long-term residents are selling their homes at an astounding rate."

"That's a good sign. The new residents won't have any knowledge of the existing church. That will work in our favor," Green affirmed.

"Good point. Gentlemen, I have prepared a take-home packet for each of you. If you open it up, just inside the first tab, you will find a skeleton outline of our strategy—nothing that would provide any evidence against us in court, of course."

Franklin chuckled. "Better to cover our tracks as we always do."

"Yes," Trent agreed. "Let's take a break for you to have desserts and look through the reports. Fresh coffee is on the way. I am available for questions for a while. I fly back to Sabal Palms in an hour."

Green hopped up and went to the dessert display. As he filled his plate up with a variety of desserts, he turned to Trent and asked, "Say, do you think you could fly us out at some point to look firsthand at the property? Don't worry. It won't make a difference in my decision, but there is nothing like walking the grounds."

"Sure. I agree. You will like what you see. We can plan for a future trip. Shirley will give you a call and set it up."

The investors, pleased with the presentation, decided to move forward with the project. They finished dessert and coffee and left shortly afterward. Trent felt like he ruled the world. That's the feeling he longed for, the feeling he craved. His goal in life was to have enough power, money, and influence to change the world to be what *he* wanted. He needed to be sought after by all the wealthiest of the wealthy. He wanted to be in *that* group. The top of the top. It was what he lived for since he was a child. But most of all, he was on a mission to change the beliefs of ignorant people. It was what he felt he was born to accomplish. He wanted to enlighten people and take their money at the same time.

Trent climbed into the limo parked in front of his building.

"Hello, Alfred."

"Mr. Fortune, how is your day going?"

"Splendid, Alfred. Just splendid."

"Wrap up another big deal?"

"You know it. And now, I'm flying back over to Texas for several days. Might even stay a week."

"Yes, sir. I will have you to the airport in record time."

"No need to hurry. I have a few notes here to catch up on while we are heading over there."

"Yes, sir."

Trent caught up on emails and messages on his phone during the fifteen-minute drive to the private airport. The limo pulled into the gate.

"Which hangar today, sir?"

"Oh, I'm taking the little plane today, the Cessna. It's in Hangar K."

"Yes, sir. You like flying your own plane."

Trent replied, "I do. It is relaxing to fly by myself. Besides, I'm sure neither of my own pilots would be interested in flying over to Texas and parking for a week."

"Yes, sir. I'll take you over to the hangar."

***

Trent landed his small plane at the private airport on the bay. He notified a taxi to pick him up and drive him to the island. He was nearly giddy as the taxi rolled along the small, bayside road. Trent watched the palms swaying along the road and could not help but smile. *This is really going to happen,* he thought. *I'm going to pull off another great deal. It's just around the corner. Who said money can't buy happiness?*

The taxi driver made good time across the causeway to the island. Although Trent's official business was in Sabal Palms, he did not have a choice but to stay in one of the newly renovated high-rise hotels on the island. But that would change soon. He would develop his own hotels. First, the inn on the golf course and, eventually, long-term plans including hotels along the beach. All in good time.

The taxi drove into the large, circular driveway lined by palm trees, hibiscus, and oleanders. Trent exited the car, retrieved his luggage, paid the driver an extra-large tip, and walked through the hotel door held open by the doorman.

The hotel lobby was a bright, open-air room. He could smell the salt air and hear the seagulls outside. It reminded him of his favorite hotel in Hawaii. But this wasn't Hawaii; it was Texas. And soon, he would help develop the island and Sabal Palms on the bay into world-class resort areas.

"Good evening, sir. May I help you?" the young Latina asked.

"Yes, reservation for Trent Fortune."

"Ah, yes, here we are. Mr. Fortune, you have the penthouse suite, oceanside view?"

"Yes. And how late will room service be available?"

"Until ten p.m. But the penthouse provides twenty-four-hour room service."

"Thank you."

"And you have a private elevator. Here is your elevator key, and here is your room key."

"Perfect. Thank you."

The clerk rang for the bellman, who ran quickly and took Trent's luggage. He then guided Trent to the private elevator. "Here you are, sir."

"Aren't you riding up with me?"

"No, sir. I will take the service elevator, and I will join you momentarily with your luggage."

In the quietness of the elaborately decorated private elevator, Trent smiled and whispered to himself, "On top of the world."

The panoramic view from the penthouse suite of the Gulf coastline was breathtaking. Trent enjoyed similar views wherever he stayed. From Hawaii to Europe to Asia, he longed for nothing at all. He was a completely self-made man. He had amassed an unbelievable net worth that included multiple homes, business properties, resorts, airplanes, yachts, and large sections of multiple small towns. But of all the investments and properties he had, he was most proud of his ability to buy old churches, remodel them, and turn them into places for New Age gatherings, such as coffee shops and bistros, and the larger churches remodeled for speakers of the truth, the New Age assemblies.

At his core, even though his parents attempted to raise him in church, he never bought into Christianity. He thought it was restrictive, old-fashioned, and unproductive. His father's cruelty made him want to run as far away as possible from Christianity. Trent knew there was no one in charge of his fate, his destiny, his achievements, but him. He was one with the universe. He was his own god.

Chapter Nine

The sea fog that had rolled in during the night made it difficult for Elaine and Bonnie to keep an eye on Bella as she dashed ahead chasing the birds she could smell but not see. Keeping up with Bella prevented them from discussing much about Trent Fortune. There were many unanswered questions, which bothered them both.

Bonnie told Elaine her own worrying was split between Trent's golf course proposal and finding out more about Mary's mystery cousin. "Why in the world hasn't this inscrutable cousin kept in touch with Mary? Is she hiding something? Why show up now after so many years? We don't know anything about her or her husband, this Charles, whoever he is. Who knows if he would be a good match for our little church? Or if they would be a good match for our community?"

Elaine agreed. "I have to admit I'm worried about it, too. Given what we discovered about Trent's possible motives, the church will require a strong leader. Whether it's Mary's cousin's husband or someone else. We need a pastor who can lead the church in the right direction and stand up to any potential bullies or people who sway vulnerable executive committee members with financial incentives."

"Uh huh," Bonnie agreed. "We need to figure out a way to let the executive committee know what Trent has done in the past."

"It would help the committee in the selection process to pick a candidate that will know how to handle the likes of him."

"Elaine, you realize the executive committee can be fooled."

"What do you mean?"

"Trent will likely offer buckets of money to that group, you know, in the form of donations."

"Good point. There are so many issues here and potential problems. We need to check out the legal process to block his plans all together if possible."

"I agree. Thanks for the walk. Helps my blood sugar, you know. I'll be over in twenty minutes to go to Adriana's house."

"Okay." Elaine turned to her dog, who was wagging her tail nonstop. "Come on, Bella."

Bonnie arrived at Elaine's cottage exactly twenty minutes later. Elaine was scurrying around gathering the notes she had made the night before. She spent more time searching the internet in the last few days than she had in years. It seemed the more she searched, the more evidence she found about Trent and his disreputable business dealings.

Elaine stuffed a few more handwritten notes in her small briefcase. "I think this is everything."

"Good." Bonnie fiddled with a cloth tote bag she had brought. "We have a long day ahead of us, so I brought some healthy snacks. For goodness' sakes, a girl doesn't want to run out of options."

Elaine laughed and locked her cottage. "Good. The sea fog is gone. Clear driving for our short trip over to Adriana's house."

"We should be there in no time," Bonnie agreed.

Elaine turned the car out onto the road, and within twenty yards, she put on the brakes. "Good grief!"

Bonnie gasped, "For heaven's sakes! What is that? What is he doing here?"

In the middle of the road, Elaine stared at the apparent invader. "Is he a surveyor? He has some kind of equipment."

"Is that what that thing is?" Bonnie asked.

"Yes. It looks like a high-class piece of equipment. My guess is laser perhaps? And he's not alone. Look." Elaine gestured.

"What's on that shirt? Can you read the shirt? They both have on green shirts beneath those orange vests."

Elaine inched the car up a few feet. "It says something, something Conversation Indus—"

Bonnie blurted, "That scoundrel! He's already surveying the land. Look, a caravan of vans down the road with different surveyors! It says Evergreen Recreation and Conservation Industries on each van."

The vans were stretched out down the road, and men, working in pairs, were scattered throughout the roadside.

Bonnie sighed. "It has begun. The selling off of properties to this . . ."

"Wealthy man?"

"Elaine, that's not what I was thinking. I was thinking more like fraud! Swindler! Trickster!" Bonnie's face was red by the time she had finished calling Trent names.

"Bonnie, watch your blood pressure. Remember, we have options. We are not finished yet."

Bonnie's mouth gaped. "Elaine! I'm shocked."

"Why?"

"You're the one who said it's out of our control; that it is all up to God. And now, here you are, trying to make plans to control things."

"Bonnie, you know the old saying: 'if God plans for you to dig a hole, you can't do it by leaning on the shovel.'"

Bonnie laughed.

Rounding the turn to Dolphin Lane three blocks before Adriana's house, Bonnie screamed, "Stop! Stop!"

Scared to death, Elaine slammed on the brakes.

"For goodness' sakes, Bonnie, what's the matter now?"

"Is that . . . Is that an alligator?"

Elaine moved the car along slowly. "It is so still. It looks fake."

"You mean, like those plastic flamingos and wooden pelicans people put in their yards?"

"Yes."

Elaine rolled the car slowly.

"It is so still. It doesn't look real," Elaine said. "Alligators don't get out of their habitats very often. I know we've had them roaming around away from water after a storm, but this would be strange this far into town."

Bonnie gestured. "Look! You can see his throat moving like he just ate something. It *is* real! I can't believe this creature is all the way in the middle of town!"

Elaine watched and determined the alligator was, indeed, moving. "Wonder what disturbed him."

"Elaine, do you think it was all those surveyors moving around back there on the road?"

"Possibly. If that's the reason this guy walked into town, it will only get worse if this project is approved."

"You're right!"

Before Elaine could say anything, Bonnie bounded out of the car with her phone and walked closer to the alligator.

Elaine put the car window down. "Good grief, Bonnie! What are you doing?"

Bonnie didn't answer. She put her phone up to her eye and began taking pictures. At that moment, the alligator charged forward. Bonnie scrambled back to the car and jumped in.

"Oh! My word, Bonnie! What were you thinking?"

"I was thinking no one would believe us without a picture! This is our proof."

"Proof?"

"That these creatures are starting to move about with all this activity near the refuge."

"Bonnie, that was good thinking. Dangerous but good."

"Mary's going to love it, don't you think? Animals being disturbed? I mean, she won't love that the animals are being disturbed, but she will be happy we can use it!"

Bonnie continued scrolling through the pictures on her phone. "I had three good photos, and one . . . well, it's a blur because he came at me, and I started moving. Messed up the shot. If I hadn't run, it would have been a closer shot."

"I think running to the car was a smart idea. That photograph might have been the *last* thing you did if you hadn't made it to the car."

Bonnie nodded.

Elaine and Bonnie walked up the steps to Adriana's house. Mary pulled her car into the driveway shortly afterward and tooted her horn. "Hello, troopers! Ready to go to battle?"

Once again, the women had a common cause. Together, they survived and rebuilt after the hurricane, and now they would bond together against this common enemy: Trent Fortune.

***

With coffee cups filled to the brim and a large plate of sweet rolls, the three sixty-somethings gathered around the younger Adriana at her kitchen table. Elaine pulled out and organized her new notes. The others placed their pages, printed yesterday, in neat stacks on the table.

"Before we start," Bonnie said, "you should know we had two encounters—first, with Trent Fortune's surveyors—

"Where?" Mary asked.

"On the road into town. All along the whole road."

Mary huffed, "Scallywag!"

"And then, we had an encounter with an alligator!"

Adriana's arms thrashed around, and her excitement could be measured by the increased decibels of the clanging of her bracelets. "What? An alligator? Here? In town? An alligator?"

"Yes. Elaine stopped the car, and I took pictures. Look." Bonnie passed her phone around.

The women gasped at the pictures.

"And then, he charged at me! Look at this messed-up photo. I was running back to the car."

"Heaven forbid!" exclaimed Mary. "You could have been killed! He could have torn you into shreds!"

"I made it back to the car, and we sped off."

"It scared me. I was afraid I'd be calling 911 instead of safely making it here," Elaine added.

Adriana handed Bonnie her phone. Putting the phone back in her purse, Bonnie asked, "Mary, do animals—you know, like alligators and others—move around when construction workers come in? Like these surveyors?"

"It is very likely. I'll bring this up at the meeting at Wildlife Refuge Center later this week. Might help our cause."

"That's what I thought. Anything to go up against that scammer."

The four women continued with a bit of small talk and continued enjoying their coffee and sweet rolls with light chatter.

Adriana broke the lighter mood and posed the most pressing question first. "Mary, before we dive into this"—she patted her stack of papers—"I have to know, what's up with your cousin? And her husband? Did you finally get to talk to her after the meeting they had at the church?"

Mary brushed a crumb from her brightly colored "Save the Ocelot" t-shirt and uncharacteristically hesitated to answer.

"Well?" Bonnie pressed.

"I am not exactly sure how to put this," Mary replied.

"You? You always say something whether it's the right way to 'put it' or not," Bonnie said.

"It's just that, well, I think she is an oddball. She is a strange bird. I've never been able to figure her out. Growing up, she was always scheming and up to no good. I was suspicious of her. If she wanted something or she wanted to go somewhere, she figured out a way, even if she got in trouble with her parents for forging ahead with her mischievous deeds."

Elaine entered the discussion. "But, Mary, how about since she has grown up?"

"I can't really say. Once we were both married, we went our separate ways. She and Charles came over last night and stayed about an hour. I don't feel any better about her, and her husband seems to be a piece of work."

"Oh?" Adriana asked.

"Spill it," Bonnie said. "Tell us everything they said. Every detail."

"I had the feeling they were playing their cards close to the chest. They were hiding something, for sure. They didn't tell me anything about their intentions, the meeting at the church with the committee, nothing. Not so much as a peep about any of that. All they did was attempt to pump me for information."

Elaine knew Bonnie could not be stopped and that Bonnie would have a stream of further questions. She was right.

"What questions? About the church? About Sabal Palms? You? What questions?" Bonnie demanded answers.

"Not much about the church at all. It was strange. They didn't ask one question about the church, Pastor Sam, or the congregation. And I told them know it was my church. Instead, they wanted to know about the people of Sabal Palms."

Elaine paused for a moment. "You know, maybe it was confidential. The committee might have asked them not to talk about it, since he might be a candidate."

Mary insisted the line of questioning was strange. "Why would someone moving into a town as a potential pastor want to know about the wealthiest people in the community? Like, strange questions. Do the wealthy people have many friends? They asked if there are many wealthy widows. And are there other family members of these affluent people in town? And do those wealthy people have children who live far away? They even knew some of the names of the wealthy. They mentioned your name, Adriana. I am telling you, they are up to no good. That is exactly how Kathy was growing up—weird. Asking questions so she could figure out how to manipulate people. She schemed me out of babysitting money one time when we were younger. Never got over that!"

The other women stared at Mary in silence.

Bonnie was the first to speak. "You're right. It seems a little whacky. No offense to you about your cousin, but maybe they're just not very smart and don't realize they are asking such nosy, intrusive questions."

Elaine couldn't contain her thoughts any longer. "This isn't very Christian of me, but maybe they *are* smart—like connivingly smart."

Bonnie announced, "Smart like foxes!"

"I know she's my cousin, but I have to agree with you. I don't trust her. And I don't trust Charles because he is married to her! I think they are partners in crime—or at least partners in something fishy."

Adriana, who had been quiet through most of the discussion, offered an intriguing question. Pointing to her head as if a lightbulb had just lit up, she said, "Wait a minute! What are the odds? I mean, Antony—God rest his soul"—signing of the cross—"didn't gamble much. But we would go to Vegas occasionally, and he liked to also play the horses sometimes. But Vegas! Loved it! I mean, in Vegas, I preferred the slot machines, and Antony like roulette. Of course, if we won, he donated it to our Catholic church—"

Mary interrupted, "Get on with it. Where were you going with this idea of odds?"

"What are the odds that this Trent Fortune fellow and your cousin's husband, who are both seeming very shady, would hit our little Sabal Palms at exactly the same time? What if—"

Elaine interjected, "They're connected?"

"I'm not about to sit by and get hoodwinked by these . . . these schmoozers! The whole lot of them! Trent Fortune and his evil company, Kathy, Charles, all of them!" Bonnie ranted.

Elaine protested, "Hold on, Bonnie. We don't know any of this yet. We just suspect or question."

Adriana threw her hands in the air and pounded the table. "Let's get to it. Let's get going with all of this. We might be the only people in the whole town of Sabal Palms fighting to find out the truth. We must figure this out. And then, we must do something about it."

The others agreed.

"Okay, let's review all of these documents. There must be something here. And, Mary, how do you feel about researching Kathy and Charles? Seeing what you can dig up?"

"I think I should. I will start by calling a few relatives who might know more about their history. I can calmly say, 'Guess who came by yesterday' and see what the others back home can tell me. I'll call my other cousins."

"Good," Bonnie said.

"Let's get to work," Elaine said.

After fifteen minutes, a knock on Adriana's door halted all progress.

"Now what?" Bonnie said.

Once again, the procession of women scampered quickly to the front door.

Adriana opened the door, surprised to see Ramon and Maria standing on her porch. "Hi Ramon, Maria."

"Sorry, ladies, but we thought we would find you here together," Roman said.

"Well, come in." Adriana opened the door wider to allow them entrance.

Maria began. "We are sorry to interrupt, but we thought we should all talk."

"No problem."

Ramon said, "Bonnie, Elaine, we wanted to tell you that the developer, Mr. Fortune—"

Bonnie grunted and rolled her eyes. "Now what's he done?"

Ramon continued, "We wanted you to know that all of the land between our house and yours, Elaine, is on the chart to be purchased for a beachside café."

"What?" Elaine said. "You mean, the lots that are zoned for houses?"

"That is just absurd!" Bonnie asserted. "Our neighborhood will become a tourist destination. We will be engulfed between the houses by . . . by—"

"Intruders!" Mary said.

"Now, we must put a stop to this," Elaine said. "Ramon, Maria, we were just organizing the actions we want to take to stop this development. Would you like to join us in this battle?"

Within five minutes, the four close friends of Sabal Palms, along with their neighbors Ramon and Maria, started a journey that would have unbelievable results.

Chapter Ten

The vivid, turquoise sky contrasted by the yellow-orange, rising sun over the Gulf and aquamarine-colored water provided an exhilarating start to Trent's morning. The panoramic view from the penthouse suite was the first of the sites he would see today. His next destination would be the church on the seashore. He wanted to see it on the ground rather than the air.

He pushed the button for his personal room service.

"Yes, Mr. Fortune, what can I get for you?"

"I would like your dark roast Kona coffee, eggs benedict, and a side of your fresh Hawaiian pineapple."

"Yes, sir. It will be there in ten minutes."

"Oh, and do you have fresh-squeezed orange juice?"

"Grown right here in the Rio Grande Valley."

"That sounds pretty amazing. Thank you."

He dressed more casually today for his excursion. He observed, during previous visits, most of the locals wore sandals or flip-flops, shorts, and casual t-shirts or short-sleeved Hawaiian-style shirts sporting tropical prints, fish, or other indications of living the tropical lifestyle. His authentic, made-in-Hawaii linen shirt; beige cargo shorts; and Tommy Bahama leather sandals would help him be less noticeable.

A knock at the door announced the arrival of his gourmet breakfast. The waiter rolled in a cart filled with delightfully displayed breakfast items and additional samples.

Gesturing to the table in front of the large oceanside window, Trent observed, "This is quite a presentation you have here."

"Sí, the chef wanted you to sample the variety of breakfast items on the especials, er, specials."

"Please give my compliments to the chef. And here's an additional tip for him as well."

"Gracias."

Enjoying the scrumptious items on the breakfast cart, Trent debated how he should travel over to Sabal Palms. Deciding a more thorough examination of Port Isabel would be helpful, he opted by taxi rather than ferry.

Trent buzzed the concierge.

"Mr. Fortune, what can I do for you?"

"Is it possible to hire a taxi or limo for the day? For sight-seeing?"

"Yes. We have a driver on standby with limo service for you."

"Perfect. In about fifteen minutes?"

"Yes, sir. He will be waiting for you just outside the front entrance."

Trent took a single, leather portfolio, with a letter-sized, yellow tablet inside, in case he needed to write anything down to research later. Exiting the revolving doors, Trent saw the limo parked outside with a driver waiting to open the back door.

"Good morning, Mr. Fortune."

"Good morning." Trent offered his hand for a handshake. "What is your name, sir?"

"Jorge Garcia."

"Nice to meet you, Jorge."

Once inside the limo, Trent said, "Jorge, just take your time driving around on the island and along the route to Sabal Palms. And if you don't mind, as we go through Port Isabel, I might ask you to stop or circle a block so I may have a closer look."

"Certainly, sir. Whatever you wish."

Trent spotted the island's favorite daytime eateries. The cars were not even able to enter into the parking lot of the Yummies Bistro. *Might want to buy them out and enlarge the parking lot,* he thought.

"Say, that looks like a popular spot."

"Yes. Best place for breakfast on the island. They serve lunch, too."

"I'm wondering, are there any churches on the island? I know there are some on the other side of the causeway."

"Yes. There are a few on the island and more on the bay side."

"Interesting. Any along the way?"

"Yes."

"Can you drive by those as well?"

"Of course."

Trent was surprised to learn there were a few churches on the island and even more in Port Isabel. "This might be more difficult than I thought," he mumbled.

"Sir?"

"Nothing. Thinking out loud."

Jorge laughed. "I do that all of the time, sir."

Crossing the causeway, Trent stated, "No matter how many times I drive across the causeway, this view always takes my breath away."

"It is a sight to see. Except the one time I drove across it, and I couldn't see it."

"What?"

"It was in the late winter, and a sea fog rolled in that was so thick once I was on the top of the bridge, I couldn't see the end of it! It really looked like a bridge to nowhere." He laughed.

"I imagine that looked pretty scary."

"Yes, sir. But you know, you can't turn around. Once you are on the bridge, you are on the bridge, stuck."

"And I suppose the ferry wouldn't run on those days?"

"No, sir. Not until the fog lifts."

Trent tucked this information away to think about later. He would need to have contingency plans in place if he had an inn full of tourists needing to go back and forth.

The drive through Port Isabel was informative. Scores of shops and restaurants along the way. Several shops were strictly aimed to target tourists who wanted nothing more than cheap souvenirs to take home. The more upscale stores and little shops served the well-off residents who required designer lighting and quality, tropical-looking furniture for their luxurious second homes on the island or the bay. That group wouldn't be the problem. The so-called "winter Texans" were in the area a few months of the year and did not have the same voting rights and privileges as the full-time residents. He wouldn't worry about trying to persuade them. He would survey the winter Texans and analyze data on how to attract more of that type of part-time resident as well as tourists to the Sabal Palms area. He liked the idea of a high turnover population. In for a few months, gone, and a different batch of tourists storm into the area in the summer, with most staying a week until the next batch descended upon the coastal towns. All these short-term visitors might be wanting to go to church while they were in town. He would make certain the little church on the shore would be advertised as *the* place to go to church while they were visiting. He would put someone in place at the church to educate the people about New Age. The summer tourists were customarily vacationers from the United States and Mexico. They, too, would be targeted as potential church-goers.

"Any place in particular you would like to go in Port Isabel?"

"Just out of curiosity, is there a block or two of town offices or centers for local business?"

"Yes. Just off Queen Isabella Boulevard on Maxim Street. I will run by there if you like."

"Thank you."

Out of the limo window, Trent observed the old lighthouse, the post office, the town office, a few restaurants, a couple of seafood markets, a furniture store, an art gallery, and a tourist area with pirate décor. "Anything special about the tourist area over there?"

"Pirate's Landing? They have a pirate ship that loads up with families and tours the bay. It's complete with a cannon on the other side that fires at the pirates. All make-believe, of course."

"Clever."

"They have tourist shops, restaurants, an ice cream shop—you name it in that general area. Oh, and an aquarium. The kids can touch starfish and look at other marine life in there."

"Might have to check that out."

These ideas were spinning in high gear through Trent's mind. He imagined he would end up owning many of these properties. And if the owners wouldn't sell, he would create even better shops and restaurants in Sabal Palms. He would take no prisoners. He was all in on this venture.

The sleepy, peaceful, little town of Sabal Palms was quite a contrast to the busier island and port areas. Sabal Palms was pristine. The gentle sea breeze was intoxicating. If only he could bottle it and sell it everywhere. He couldn't explain the magical quality of the air, the gently swaying palms, and the year-round fragrances. No doubt, the lifetime residents felt the same way. But money might entice them to sell out. Last year's hurricane helped his cause. Many were motivated to sell and move elsewhere. And all of this was about to fall right into his lap. His plan was perfectly timed to get the most land for the cheapest price.

"Jorge, I would like to go see the church on the shore."

"Yes, sir. One of my favorite places. My family visits there with our friends. But we attend the Catholic church in Port Isabel as our home church."

"And what are your thoughts about the church on the shore? Does it have a large congregation?"

"No. It varies. When the winter Texans are in town, there are more people who attend. But most of the year, it's pretty small."

"Interesting. I was not aware that winter Texans had homes in Sabal Palms."

"Only a few. Most have places on the island or Port Isabel. There are one or two on Dolphin Lane and a couple on Amberjack. I have taken them to and from the airport."

"Of course. That makes sense."

Trent felt a sense of wonder when he saw the tiny church on the shore. It looked smaller, for some reason, on the ground than it did in the drone film footage. The quaintness of the old church could not be detected from the sky.

"Think I'll get out and look around."

"Yes, sir. I can come with you if you like, in case anyone is inside— for an introduction."

"That might be helpful. Thank you."

Like most places on the island and Sabal Palms, the inside of the church was surprisingly bright and airy. There was only a single aisle with two large rows of pews on either side. Trent guessed the seating would hold three-hundred people. And that was being generous. The entire structure was practically wall-to-ceiling windows. Palm trees were visible through every window.

"Jorge, what are the birds there, outside the window?"

Jorge laughed. "I guess you didn't know that Sabal Palms is a well-known birding area. That one on the branch of the larger tree is a yellow-headed parrot. The yellow-breasted one on the railing of the back courtyard is a Kiskadee. And that one, down on the ground eating that orange set out for him, is a green jay."

"It has a blue head?"

"Yes."

"Looks like a blue jay, but it's green. Interesting."

Studying the variety of birds out of the window gave Trent another idea for a target market. Birders. They travel everywhere looking for birds all times of the year.

"And I am supposing you have migratory birds, also. You know, the ones that just pass through?"

"Oh, yes. The hummingbirds are my favorite. And you might not know, but the butterflies migrate here as well."

"Really? I didn't know that."

"I have seen hundreds of monarchs fluttering in my own backyard."

"And do you live in Sabal Palms?"

"No. We live in Port Isabel. In the older neighborhood."

This guy is a wealth of information, Trent thought. And the marketing packages were increasing. Nature packages, birding packages, golf packages. His investors would be pleased.

Not one person made an appearance in the church. Trent walked the entire interior and exterior undisturbed. His brain was full, and he needed to assimilate it all.

"Jorge, I didn't notice as we drove through town. Does Sabal Palms have a coffee shop?"

"Yes, indeed."

"Think I would like to spend some time in there making some notes. Do you mind dropping me off for a while?"

"No, sir. I need to fill up this car, and you can just call me when you are ready for me to pick you up."

"Okay. Oh, but first"—already knowing the answer—"are there houses right on the beach here?"

"Yes. A handful. Good people."

"You know them?"

"I know Ramon. I know the others, but I am not as close with them. Would you like to see those homes?"

"Is it possible to see from the road?"

"Maybe just a part of the homes. They have long driveways from the main road."

"That's okay. I wouldn't want to disturb them." Trent had seen the homes by zooming in on the drone footage. He thought he might go see the homes on foot in the future. He could appear as a wayward tourist in swimwear. But that would be another day.

***

Jorge drove the limo directly to the coffee shop in the old town area of Sabal Palms. The shops along the way were decorated with sidewalk flower boxes full of tropical plants. There were wooden pelicans by the front doors of several shops. Tiny twinkle lights were in the storefront windows. Most of the shops had flowerpots or flower boxes with large tropical plants and ferns. The sidewalks and streets were free from debris. It could be the perfect movie setting for a story in a quaint bayside town. There were a few people milling about. Most of the pedestrians knew each other and stopped to chat.

Typical small town, he thought. *Everybody knows everybody.*

***

Taking his seat in the corner of the coffee shop, Trent sat an angle to help hide from anyone who might recognize him from the town meeting. The coffee was delicious. He opened his portfolio and began to write down notes on everything he had seen and heard on his brief tour of Port Isabel and Sabal Palms. He included ideas for marketing and observational notes about the shops and other services offered in Port Isabel and Sabal Palms. He was finishing up the last sentence when the bell on the door of the coffee shop alerted him to incoming customers.

The barista behind the counter greeted the customer. "Good morning, Elizabeth. Regular?"

"Yes, thank you."

"I heard the church interviewed a couple of candidates this week for the position of pastor?"

"Just one so far. We have another one scheduled for next week."

"Was the first one a good match?"

"Not sure yet. He was a little . . . progressive for our church."

"Oh? From around here?"

"No. Somewhere out west. Oregon, I think—or was it Washington State? Well, anyway, you get the idea. From far away."

"Wonder why he wants to move all the way over here."

"Didn't say. But I think his wife may have a relative here."

"That is understandable. When our local people brag about living in our picturesque seaside town, everyone in the family wants to visit or move in!"

"Isn't that the truth! People say relatives show up that they didn't know they had."

Both women laughed and continued with the small talk. But sitting at the table in the back with his head turned to the side, barely able to control his joy, a grin spread across Trent Fortune's face.

Chapter Eleven

Another meeting to stop Trent Fortune and Evergreen Recreation and Conservation Industries convened at Adriana's house. The coffee pot was full; the army brigade of four soldiers and two new recruits was ready; and Mary and Bonnie brought additional sweet rolls and coffee cakes along with healthy lunch salad ingredients to keep the troops fortified. Adriana, charged with the dinner assignment, had already ordered a delivery of an assortment of healthy entrées from which each would pick their favorite. Maria and Ramon brought fresh tomatoes and a bag of Mexican coffee beans to add to the fortifications. The six knew it would take the entire day to come up with a solid working plan.

Elaine took out her additional research papers she had collected the night before. "By the way, Mary, did you find out anything else about your cousin and her husband?"

Before Mary started with her research details, she informed Ramon and Maria about her long-lost cousin, Kathy, and her husband, Charles.

"And new details? Oh, mercy, yes! I was on the phone all night. I called every cousin, long-lost relative, all my childhood friends, and neighbors of friends."

"Oh! Tell us!" Bonnie clapped her hands.

"Turns out they are quite a pair."

"How do you mean?" Adriana asked.

"They have been conspiring in Washington State for years. The area where these two were living is a very progressive place. The people who live there are becoming, well, shall we say, interested in other things besides the Christian church. These two knuckleheads spend their time recruiting people into their New Age religion. They are New Age con artists. They target the wealthy. Most of the family members I spoke with said these two were too scandalous for them, and they no longer associated with them. And the other family members said they avoided them for the past several years. A couple of people I spoke with said they had heard only bad things."

"Mary, I am sorry to hear this about your cousin," Elaine said.

"Thank you, Elaine, but I'm not really surprised. Kathy has been at it since she was a kid. Always trying to take advantage of people and their money. She didn't have a very good home, and it shows."

"It is another piece of the puzzle, ladies," Bonnie said.

"Oh, my stars!" Adriana exclaimed. "The whole world is plotting against poor, little Sabal Palms. Trent and his unscrupulous company and now these con artists masquerading as a pastor and his trusty wife. To think they are all conspiring to change the church. Unreal."

Ramon added, "The last few days, when I get up in the morning, I ask Maria, 'Is this really happening? Are we going to end up being a tourist town?'"

"I can't believe it either," Maria agreed.

"We have our hands full, no doubt about it. Shall we get to work?" Elaine prompted.

The women began the task at hand at nine that morning. Papers were shuffling; pencils were scratching on paper; and each one read aloud what they deemed the most important item to consider and then discussed how they would act upon each issue.

They were elbow-deep in papers and coffee cups when the doorbell rang.

Adriana threw her hands up in the air, as she customarily did. "I have no clue whatsoever who that might be. I'm expecting no one at all."

"Package delivery?" Mary asked.

"Not even that."

Adriana walked to her front door with the other three women on her heels, while Maria and Ramon remained in the kitchen shuffling through more papers. She opened the door slowly.

"Hello, Adriana."

"Yes?"

"Sorry to bother you. Uh, Thomas Williams."

"Yes?"

"Your neighbor. Next door."

"I'm sorry, Thomas. I was so busy in the kitchen. It took me a minute to collect my thoughts and to recognize you."

"May I come in for a moment?"

"Certainly. Do you know Elaine, Bonnie, and Mary?"

"Hello. I saw you ladies at the townhall meeting the other day."

"Yes," Elaine said.

Bonnie and Mary nodded.

"Uh, do you mind if I speak with Adriana alone? Just some business matters."

"Of course," Elaine said. "We'll wait in the sunroom."

Once out of earshot, Bonnie and Mary could not be stopped. They whispered back and forth.

Bonnie started. "What do you suppose that traitor wants?"

Mary whispered, "He's probably going to start pressuring her. You mark my words. This is gonna get ugly before all is said and done. He is a . . . a defector! And he's not gonna play nice. You watch."

Fearing Thomas would hear them, Elaine warned, "Girls, shhh! He might hear you."

Elaine was worried Mary and Bonnie might be right. "You both know there is a process, and we are going to try everything possible to stop it from happening. And besides, Adriana doesn't have to sell."

"It scares me. This might be getting out of control," Bonnie said.

"We're not going down that road," Elaine warned. "We are going to fight this."

Adriana entered the sunroom. "He's gone."

Ramon and Maria joined the group.

"What did he say?" Bonnie asked.

Mary asked, "What did he want?"

"He came over to tell me how excited he was about selling to Trent Fortune. He said he offered him more money than the property is worth."

Mary gasped. "What? For part of his yard?"

"No. He is selling the whole property—house, pool, everything—and moving."

Bonnie said, "Wait. What?"

"Yes. That's why he came by. He said he didn't need to list the house and that he would be packing up and moving in a few weeks. He encouraged me to listen to Trent. Thomas said Trent is a very successful businessman and that this would be good for Sabal Palms."

"Just what we were afraid of," Ramon said.

Mary blurted, "Oh, baloney! Why does he even care about Sabal Palms if he is leaving anyway? Traitor! Turncoat!"

"But he isn't leaving Sabal Palms."

"You mean, he is selling just to move somewhere in town?" Bonnie asked.

"Yes. He's going to move into a larger place two blocks away."

"Good grief!" Mary said. "He is selling *only* to help Trent move forward."

"Remember what Trent said? Thomas is the reason Trent was interested in Sabal Palms in the first place," Elaine said.

With her bracelets jangling louder than ever, Adriana pointed out what had just become obvious. "That snake-in-the-grass Trent! Now Thomas and Trent are good buddies! They are in this together. They will be a force to be reckoned with!"

"That does it. Enough is enough!" Elaine said. "The time has come to call in reinforcements. We need more people. We need the community to get behind this."

Mary interjected, "You mean it's time?"

Puzzled, Ramon asked, "Time? For what?"

Elaine nodded. "Yes. It is time to bring in Gladys and a few others. Let's get everyone asking questions about what is going on. We will plan a meeting of a few additional people. Adriana, your pool party we were planning for next week just got moved up to tomorrow evening, and it is now a community planning event."

"Elaine, what about an attorney?" Bonnie questioned.

"I think we are going to need one," Ramon agreed.

"Yes. That's it. I'm calling Billy Wrangle right now. Let's see what he says about contacting someone."

"He should know somebody," Maria said.

They absorbed every word Elaine said while on the phone with Billy. They only heard one side of the conversation, which was basically, "Yes, of course, that's a great idea . . . You would? . . . Yes, I think we could do that outside . . . I will check. How about day after tomorrow? . . . You will be ready? . . . That is a good point . . . Okay. Talk to you in a while."

Once Elaine hung up the phone, the questions spurted right out of the group.

Mary was first. "Well? What did he say? Should we get an attorney?"

"Yes. And he recommended a couple who work in Texas and Tennessee."

Bonnie followed. "And what is this great idea?"

"Oh! The best part! He volunteered to hold a free concert and take up donations to help pay for the attorney's fees. And he wants to do it day after tomorrow."

"That will go a long way to help with expenses," Ramon said.

Adriana clapped her hands and started her typical communicative hand gestures. That is fantastic! I can't believe it! Billy is . . . well, he is perfectly adorable! I am shocked! And so excited. My stars!"

Mary posed another question. "Elaine, does he want an outdoor concert?"

"Yes."

"And you need to check on . . . "

"A permit. I need to ask Mayor Townsend if we need a permit. And where do you girls think we should have this concert?"

"I can call the mayor. I finished some work for his house not long ago," Ramon said.

"Perfect," Elaine said.

"The beach? Hey, he could sing at the gazebo on the south end of the beach," Mary said.

"That is an excellent idea!" Elaine said.

"Wait!" Adriana yelled with hands in the air. "I'm having a gathering tomorrow night, and Billy's concert is only a couple of days from now?"

Bonnie's eyes bulged, "Can we get everything done in the short amount of time?"

Always looking on the bright side, Elaine cheered them on. "I know we can! We are a stronger force than those . . .

"Scammers?" Bonnie suggested.

Not wanting to engage in any further name-calling, Elaine calmly said, "'If God is for us, who can be against us?'"[1]

"Yes!" Bonnie said.

"Absolutely!" Mary added. Then she said, "Elaine, Billy said something else at the end, I think. You said it was a good point?"

"Oh, yes, he is coming over to help us plan in just—"

The doorbell interrupted Elaine's comment. She added, "Five minutes."

"I think he's here," Adriana said, walking to the front door. "Billy, come in, we are in the kitchen."

"Good morning, Adriana. I thought I should see first-hand what we are dealing with here."

Billy entered the foyer. Closing her door, she saw her neighbor, Thomas Williams, knocking on the door across the street. "What do you suppose he's doing?"

---

1   Romans 8:31

Billy looked at Thomas and said, "My guess? He's campaigning."

"Campaigning?"

"Yes. I'm thinking he's campaigning for his cause."

"You mean Trent's cause?"

"Exactly."

"Oh! That double-crosser! Oh! I'm sorry, Billy. Come this way."

In the kitchen, they could hear bracelets clanging and knew something was wrong.

"Good morning, Billy," they chimed in unison.

"Ladies," he said, removing his hat. He extended his hand to Ramon and nodded to Maria.

"Adriana, is something wrong?" Mary asked.

"Yes, I think so. We saw Thomas. I think he is going door to door."

Billy added, "I think he is campaigning to win the other neighbors over to his side of the argument."

"Horsefeathers!" Mary blasted.

"This has to be stopped," Ramon said. Ramon explained to Billy that Trent intended to put the café right on the beach.

"We have to put a halt to this," Adriana said.

Elaine turned to Billy and asked, "Would you like some coffee or a bite to eat?"

Adriana said, "Oh, goodness me! Where are my manners? Billy, please, help yourself to these treats, and I will pour you some coffee."

"Nothing to eat, but coffee would be great."

As Billy sipped his coffee, Elaine brought him up to speed on the town and county regulations and the general process. Mary, Adriana, and Bonnie reviewed the documents. Elaine concluded, "And this is why we think we need a lawyer."

"You're right. These large corporations stop at nothing. But I think you need to do a couple of other things."

"Oh?" Elaine questioned.

"Yes," Billy continued. "I know you are gathering a group tomorrow night here, Adriana. And with that group, we will need to start our own campaign right away. In doing so, they can spread the word about the concert to increase attendance. The more we get to show up, the greater our funds."

"And is there another thing we need to do?" Bonnie asked.

"Well, I have another suggestion," Billy added. "I believe you need a bigger cause. Right now, your cause is to block the development all together. You all want to block it for financial reasons and for personal reasons—"

"And because we don't want our church turning into a New Age meeting hall," Elaine added.

"Or people all over the beach ruining it," piped in Bonnie.

"Yes. But not everyone in the community attends that little church or goes to the beach. There may be some who agree with you about both issues, but it might not rally all the people together. We need a cause that the people who live here can get behind in case they attend another church, don't care about the beach, or aren't familiar with the differences between New Age and Christianity. Let's think—"

Before he could finish his sentence, Mary blurted, "Ocelots!"

"Ocelots?" Adriana questioned.

"Yes! They are a protected species. And do you know what the biggest threat to this particular species is?"

"No clue," Bonnie said.

"Land development. The new development in the area clears away their habitat. And by building this extensive golf course right up to and including part of the refuge, it takes away their home, where they sleep and live with their babies. Fewer places to live, fewer ocelots."

"Mary, that's perfect!" Billy said smiling. "We can get the people at the wildlife refuge involved."

"Absolutely. And all the animal activist groups support each other. The birders, the marine life groups—all of them. They will jump on board."

"I know many of those people. I work with them, and I agree—they will join us," Ramon said.

"This is great news," Billy said. "Any of you know where we might get some graphics made? We need to develop the flyers and brochures right away. Elaine, can you take care of writing up the paragraphs to go with the graphics?"

"I would be happy to. And as for the graphics, I believe there are some cards posted in the coffee shop of freelancers in the area."

"How about I run over and grab those and come back?" Billy volunteered. "We can get started this morning. Hopefully by this afternoon, we'll have some drafts to look over; and by Adriana's meeting tomorrow evening, we will have these brochures and flyers ready to hand out. At the bottom of each, we will announce the concert. And we can add a specific flyer for the concert as well."

"Okay, Billy, while you're doing that, I will go to the mayor's office and talk about the permit for the concert. I think we can get it approved before we print those flyers," Ramon said.

Billy gave him the thumbs up. "Great!"

Elaine said, "Bonnie and Mary, I'm sure Adriana would appreciate help in planning the meeting for tomorrow. We'll need a short agenda and who will be speaking. Also, a grouping by neighborhoods of who will take which blocks to campaign. Adriana, once the guest list is made, we can start calling each one to invite them over."

"On it," Adriana said.

Elaine looked at Billy and Ramon and asked, "Meet back here for lunch?" Elaine asked.

All agreed.

Chapter Twelve

Trent sat in his penthouse waiting for his room service dinner to be delivered. Gazing over the aquamarine Gulf waters, he savored the setting sun casting pink, violet, and orange streaks across the sky. The reflection on the few small cumulus clouds added brilliance to the already picturesque view. The knock at the door interrupted his peaceful daydreaming.

"Room service, Mr. Fortune."

"Ah, please come in."

Trent opened the door and gestured toward the large dining table set before the floor to ceiling windows.

"How are you today, Mr. Fortune?"

"Very good, very good."

The waiter set the dishes filled with seafood, salads, and fresh fruits and vegetables on the table along with a formal setting of china, crystal, and silver. He added the linen napkin and lit two candles. "And, sir, you did not request dessert, so we added a small dessert tray with several options in case you wanted to taste these. And here's a fresh pot of coffee."

"Thank you. This will be wonderful."

"On your bill, sir?"

"That will be fine. And please add a twenty-five percent tip for you and another tip for the chef."

"Yes, sir."

Trent ate the delectable meal and continued his fantasy of his newfound pot of gold at the end of the rainbow. He believed Sabal Palms and his creations of a golf course, restaurants, and other tourist attractions would generate more money than any of his other investments. That was his financial goal. His other goals about the churches in the area would be more difficult, but he felt certain he could reach those as well.

His plan was simple. He would either persuade the church on the shore to allow him to remodel and reopen the church to his liking, or he would use under-the-table methods to have the property condemned. "And the power of our new religion will spread over the region," he said with a smile.

Trent decided to stay a few more days in Sabal Palms before he flew back to pick up the investors. He knew their impressions of the town and the island would increase their desire to own as much of this area as possible.

Trent called the front desk. "Yes, hello. Can you arrange for Jorge to take me around the island, the port, and other areas in the morning?"

"Yes, of course, Mr. Fortune."

Tomorrow, Trent would outline the specific route he would take his investors.

***

Dressed in casual clothes, Trent walked from the front door of the hotel to the limo. He carried a bag packed with a swimsuit and flip-flops.

"Good morning, Mr. Fortune," Jorge said opening the door.

"Good morning, Jorge."

"Where would you like to go today?"

"Well, Jorge, I am going to have some business partners in town in a few days, and today, I would like to be sure I know where to take them."

"I see."

"It's important for these investors to see a variety of the tourist places we saw yesterday. And today, I want to be absolutely certain about the location of the churches, Port Isabel sight-seeing and tourist shops, the beach at Sabal Palms, and the church on the shore."

"Sí, yes. First, I will take you by the churches on the island if you like."

"That would be great."

The bright sunlight on the dingy brown, brick exterior of the first church Jorge drove to was a stark contrast to the typical beach feeling of the other buildings. The structure itself was old, probably one of the oldest buildings on the island. The stained-glass windows instantly took him back in time to his childhood church days, and as if he was caught in a time warp of some kind, he was back on the sidewalk walking with his parents. He was six years old when his parents lectured him outside the old church in front of their friends and the pastor. He would never forget the pain in the pit of his stomach as they ranted on publicly. He was restless, rowdy, and could not remain quiet or still for five minutes, much less for an entire sermon. Not only did his hyperactivity cause friction within the home and school environments, but he also suffered each Sunday with the lectures, humiliation, and punishment at home afterwards. His father could be downright abusive. At the time,

Trent didn't understand about being an abused child. He only knew that when his father started drinking, he couldn't stop whipping him with the leather belt. His mother had rushed in and tried to stop his father. But his father had continued, nonetheless, and left Trent with a mountain of hate toward him.

The buckle marks would be treated with ointment by his mother after the fact. Usually, just one or two lines, where the metal broke through his skin and caused him to bleed. The bruises were much larger. She told Trent many times, "Your father is a good man. He doesn't mean to hit you this hard. He just can't control himself. He just wants you to be the best man you can be when you grow up."

But Trent knew it was the alcohol that caused the temper. And every Sunday, his father would go to church, say confession with the rest of the congregation, and believe he was clean and could start all over again for another week.

This is why Trent didn't believe anything he had heard in church as a child. His parents bought the whole fairytale the pastor told each Sunday. The pastor would preach forgiveness for all sins. And each Sunday, Trent fidgeted, squirmed, and made noises just to get through the more-than-hour-long sermon. He had vowed then and there he would never believe in that garbage.

He tolerated the church fairytales each week and eventually was able to make it through the services by thinking about other things. The beatings eased up when Trent was older and sat still for the lengthy sermons. In high school, his thoughts deliberately wandered during church to what he would become as an adult. He would show his father. He would find a place in society. He didn't care if his father was proud or not. He would make ten times the income of his father. Maybe more. His goals were set on making money—lots of money—and leaving the small, Georgia town where his parents still lived. He would be somebody important. He would certainly be more important than his father.

Unlike other high school boys back then, he was not athletic and was more interested in learning the stock market than learning a girl's phone number. He had to make money when he was young so he could keep making more and more money. He knew once he was wealthy, he would have time for women. He would do whatever he wanted.

It was not until he was in college that he learned about other types of religions. He disavowed all tenants of Christianity and embraced Eastern beliefs, New Age religion, and even dabbled a bit in satanical cults and sects. But he had settled in the New Age beliefs because he felt relief from Christianity. He liked thinking that God is everything and everything is God. He felt a free-flowing spirit and no guilt, no responsibility, and no worry about having to help other people. He had helped himself. Other people should do that, too.

He prided himself in telling others about these beliefs. He brought new believers into this religion. Sometimes, he even told eager achievers that his religion was the religion of money. He especially enjoyed talking to Christians, who were poor and weak, and turning them into believers of New Age. He told them he was once poor, too. But this new way of believing—practically worshipping money—was attractive to those who struggled. When they listened to Trent, they left the Christian church in droves.

He remodeled churches and made the exterior and interiors more like meeting rooms for people to talk about such things as being their own god or using crystals for drawing negative energy away and attracting positive energy from the universe. He treasured painting the interiors and exteriors of the buildings with murals of stars, planets, the ocean, and abstract designs. He made some of the small, old churches into coffee shops, where the members could discuss astrology, being their own inner god, energy, and all matters of spirituality without ever mentioning archaic topics like the Bible, crucifixion, or Easter or even singing old hymns. Trent knew he could turn larger churches into buildings where New Age speakers and prophets of all varieties could be brought in to dazzle New Age believers.

Remodeling these old churches had other wonderful outcomes as far as Trent was concerned. One outcome was to have one less building where Christians would worship. One less church where some poor schmuck would believe he had been saved. And to have one more place where visitors, mostly Christians, would accidentally wander in, thinking they would hear a sermon but would instead hear the truth. He wanted to enlighten the universe with the fact that each human was one with the universe, that every person was their own god.

"Mr. Fortune?"

"Oh, Jorge, I'm sorry. I was thinking about a different church."

"Would you like to go inside, sir? I know the preacher here."

"Certainly. If you think it is okay."

Once inside, Trent's stomach knotted up as it did when he was a boy. He had to get out of this old place. The inside even smelled like his parents' church.

"Looks like Pastor Mark is not here. But the choir is meeting in the front. Would you like to stay and listen?"

"Oh, no, thank you. We can continue with the tour around the island."

**

The experience of the old church knocked Trent off his game. He felt a little off-balance and needed to collect himself. "Say, Jorge, is there a coffee shop on the island?"

"Yes, it is about a mile north of here. Would you like to go?"

"That would be wonderful."

Jorge pulled the car into the parking lot.

"Jorge, would you like a cup?"

"No, thank you. I'll wait here."

The small coffee shop, Café Karma, offered a variety of coffees, sweets, and ice cream. A few other customers sat at small tables. Trent ordered a coffee and sat off to the side. He took out his tablet and wrote several notes of places he wanted to visit.

His mind wandered back again to the old church he had just visited. He wished he hadn't gone there. He was not prepared for that embarrassing memory and the torture of his thoughts. Why did it bother him so much? After so many years, why now? His cuts and bruises were healed long ago. But not his spirit.

Glancing at his phone and checking the time, he closed his leather portfolio and returned to the car.

The tour continued as Trent had requested. He wrote down every detail and examined each shop, town office, and church with scrutiny. He spoke with shop owners who believed he was a tourist.

After each stop, he wrote detailed notes in his portfolio about the type of inventory and a guess as to the value of the property and a separate, detailed estimate of the value of the business. He could buy them all out if he chose.

Once in Sabal Palms, he grew anxious to walk on the beach. He wanted to examine it as a new tourist who had just placed flip-flops on his feet and walked along the shore.

"Jorge, I want to walk a bit on the beach. Is there a place you can park for a while?"

"Yes. I think I can just park in the church parking lot."

"That will work. I know it's getting late, so I won't be long."

***

The meeting at Adriana's house wrapped up with a firm plan for their next steps. The gathering soon to follow at Adriana's house was outlined in detail. Each member of the seven-member brigade to stop Trent Fortune had their marching orders. The phone tree was established. The community would soon know what was happening. They would each have an opportunity to fight back.

But before any of those plans could materialize, an unexpected turn of events was about to happen.

"We are all set?" Elaine asked.

"Yes. We will start our phone calls tonight and invite the main community organizers to the meeting at Adriana's house. Everyone would be told about the concert," Mary said.

"And the brochures for the concert will be ready for pick up at ten a.m. tomorrow. Then I will post them all over town," Mary said.

"And we will stop by the Coastal Grocery tomorrow morning and talk to Gladys."

Once all plans were finalized, the group departed and went their separate ways. Elaine and Bonnie were soon back at the beach.

"Should we go ahead and get a quick walk in?" Elaine asked.

"That sounds great. Sitting all day long is not good for old people." Bonnie laughed. "My feet look like fat sausages."

"I'll just get Bella. She has been inside all day."

Bella gladly tagged along as they walked the shoreline.

"All of this"—Bonnie gestured out to the water—"will be unrecognizable. There will be herds of children and, worse, potentially spring-breakers—"

"Heaven forbid! Spring-breakers in our own front yard!" Elaine interrupted. "Let's hope not!"

The sand was still hot from the afternoon sun, and Bella hopped over to the cooler wet sand.

"Made it this year without a hurricane," Bonnie observed.

"Wait. The season isn't over yet. It isn't over until the end of November."

"That seems like a long time from now."

Elaine agreed. "In some ways, it does. But it's only a few weeks away, and we have a lot to do between now and then."

"Yes. Well, this is where I leave you two," Bonnie said, turning to her cottage.

"See you tomorrow."

Elaine and Bella continued toward the aqua-and-white cottage. Looking on the image with the sun's last rays casting shadows, Elaine remembered how the cottage had looked after Jada. It was a sight.

Thankfully, Carlos was able to repair all the damage to her cottage and rebuild Bonnie's within a few months.

Elaine was lost in her thoughts when a tall, shadowy figure startled her.

"Hi," the man said.

"Hello?"

"Elaine, is it? Elaine Smith? Trent Fortune," the man reminded her.

"Oh, hi. Yes, you startled me."

"Sorry. Just walking along the shore. I was down at the old church and decided to walk for a while."

Elaine felt the knots in her stomach right away. *Now what?* she wondered.

"Say, what do you know about the old church?" he asked.

"I'm not exactly sure what you are asking."

"Do a lot of people go there? I mean, it's pretty old, and I was wondering about it."

"Many of my friends go there. I do, too."

Trent paused for a moment. "Is it a Methodist or Baptist or Lutheran church?"

She laughed. "No. It is a Christian church. Denomination doesn't matter. Just as long as you believe in Christ and that He is your Savior, that church is for you."

"I see. And you believe this?"

"I do. I know He died for my sins."

"That makes you feel good? That some man died for you?"

"I don't believe He was just *some* man, and I feel awful about Him sacrificing His life for anyone. He had done no wrong. But I know that His death covered my sins. I know I can go to Him with my confession, and I can ask Him for help any time."

"Guess I don't quite understand all of that stuff. Doesn't really make sense to me."

Not certain what to say next, Elaine simply added, "You should come and hear the message on Sunday. And if you want to know more, I would be happy to talk with you about it."

Looking like he couldn't get away fast enough from any further conversation about Christianity, Trent said, "No, I think I'm good. Nice talking with you."

Trent continued on his way toward Ramon's cottage. Elaine watched as he went past Ramon's house and went further north up the shore.

Elaine walked back up the steps to her cottage. She didn't know what to think. Should she have confronted Trent right then about his plans? *Better to wait until our ducks are in a row.*

"Come on, Bella. Let's go inside."

Chapter Thirteen

Even though she had worked past midnight the night before on a story about bringing non-believers to Christ, Elaine was up before sunrise. She was upset by the comments Trent made implying that Christ was just some random man. It was difficult for her to understand there were people in the world who believed that very statement. What could be done to bring these people to the Truth?

She and Bella met Bonnie for their morning walk. A few steps into the walk, Elaine couldn't contain her thoughts about Trent. She had to tell Bonnie. "You won't believe what happened to me."

"Of course, I will. Spill it. What?"

"He was here last night. On the beach."

"Who?"

"Trent Fortune."

"What?" Bonnie grunted. "What was he doing? Did you talk to him?"

"It was right after you went inside. At first, I only saw a man's silhouette because of the angle of the sun. Then out of nowhere, he spoke to me. He startled me when he said hi."

"Who does he think he is? Walking around on our beach."

"But that's just it. It *isn't* our beach. This strip of sand here"— Elaine waved her hand over the beach—"belongs to no one. Anybody can be here."

"Scoundrel of a man. He wants to commercialize our beautiful place," Bonnie said, gesturing out over the bay.

"That's not all."

"Can't possibly be worse."

"It is, unfortunately."

"What?"

"He asked about the church. He said he started his walk on the beach from the church."

"What did that greedy, nosy man want to know?"

"He asked how many people went to the church, and then he asked me if I felt bad knowing that some 'man' had died for me."

"Piffle! Gibberish! I have never heard such!" Then Bonnie used air quotes with her fingers. "A 'man'? That just shows what a buffoon he is. Good grief. We have to do something."

"We are. We are going to stop him."

Bonnie stopped walking, turned, and looked at Elaine. "We have to tell Pastor Sam."

"But Pastor Sam will be moving to his new church in one more week," Elaine said.

Elaine insisted. "We have to tell him just the same. He must tell the executive committee. Everyone in the church will need to resist this invasion of false prophecy. We can also call Elizabeth Randolf. She is on my list of people to call this morning. She can call the executive committee members."

"You're right. We can't wait any longer. You and I will arrange to see Pastor Sam today. First thing after breakfast, I'll call the church."

"Deal. Let's go get breakfast at my place; then we can go over to the church."

***

Once breakfast was consumed and Elaine and Bonnie had regrouped their thoughts, Elaine walked back to her own cottage and dressed to meet Pastor Sam. They were fortunate that he was available and already at the church packing his office.

Elaine knocked on Bonnie's door.

"Come on in. About ready."

"Okay. I left the car running with the AC on. Already getting warm today."

"Good. Hate to have an unpleasant aroma surrounding us when we get to church. Let's go."

The distance to the church was short but just long enough to cause a solid sweat if the women went on foot.

Pastor Sam saw the car pull into the parking lot from his office window and greeted the women at the front door. "Good morning, ladies. Please, come in from this heat."

"Good morning, Pastor," Elaine replied.

"Let's just have a seat here in the sanctuary. My office is a mess of boxes."

Elaine and Bonnie sat behind the pastor, who turned to face them. "Now, what brings you young ladies by so early in the morning?"

"We wanted to talk with you about Trent Fortune."

"Oh, he is going to do great things in our community."

"Well, there is something you don't know about him," Elaine said. She proceeded to relay her conversation with Trent on the beach and then added everything she knew from her research.

Pastor Sam's eyes grew wider as he listened. He was silent for a few moments and then responded, "I am so sorry to hear of this news.

It places the church in an unusual position. The timing, of course, couldn't be worse. The congregation will be left without a pastor in a week's time. But we are interviewing—"

Bonnie interrupted, "Yes, we heard. And there is more to that story as well."

"Oh? What's that?" Pastor Sam asked.

Bonnie replied, "The candidate from out west, Oregon or wherever—"

"Charles? Seemed to be a fine fellow."

Bonnie continued, "He is another wolf in sheep's clothing. He is one of these New Age types. We think he and Trent are connected."

"But we don't have any proof yet," Elaine added.

"Oh, dear. This is bad. Who would ever have believed someone—a false prophet, if you will—would be coming here to Sabal Palms? To our little 'Church on the Shore'?"

"Exactly," Elaine continued. "Is there something we can do?"

"You don't worry about a thing. I will talk to the executive committee. I will call them in for a meeting this morning."

Relieved, Elaine said, "Thank you, Pastor Sam."

Elaine and Bonnie stood to leave.

"Oh, one more thing," Pastor Sam said.

"Yes?" the women said simultaneously.

"The concert tomorrow night is a wonderful idea. I wouldn't miss it."

***

Elaine and Bonnie returned to their own cottages to continue the task of calling each name on their respective phone tree list. Elaine knew her task was to get everyone in town on board with their plan to resist the development planned by Trent Fortune and his organization. She also knew she needed to make sure the townspeople would show up at the concert. It was a monumental task.

The small group of workers would add Gladys to their informal committee today. Gladys would spread the news quickly. Although Gladys would not be able to attend their planning meeting this afternoon because of work, she would fulfill the necessary role on the ground of blasting the news all over town. What's more, Elaine knew Gladys would complete this task with respect, and all who heard the news would be convinced it was their duty to attend the concert.

The informal working group had agreed to stay at their own homes this morning and call their designated list of people on their phone tree. After making their phone calls, Mary and Adriana would go together, door to door, to talk with their neighbors. It was important to have the main community influencers—those on church committees, volunteers at the animal rescue centers, the tropical gardening club, and workers in town—on board with the plan. Several would be invited to the gathering at Adriana's house. It would all come together; Elaine could sense it.

Elaine, Bonnie, Ramon, and Maria would join Adriana and Mary after lunch and report anyone they failed to contact and come up with plans to reach each person. They would examine and expand the agenda for the meeting at Adriana's house to be held later that evening. And their final task of the day would be to assemble all needed supplies, including snacks, and take these to Adriana's before four o'clock. They had planned a light dinner together to finalize their plans.

***

Elaine left her cottage and drove to Bonnie's to pick her up. She collected Bonnie, and they piled the additional supplies for the meeting in the back seat.

"Running a little late, are you?" Bonnie smirked.

"Oh, I got carried away."

"For Pete's sakes, what were you doing?"

"Going over my notes. I have quite a bit I want to discuss with the group. We all need to be on the same page."

"Yes, we do. We are up against a monster, after all."

"I can't help but think there is more to his story, like something that caused him to be such a skeptic," Elaine said.

"Whose story?"

"Trent Fortune, of course."

"Now, don't start feeling sorry for him. Good grief. He is a selfish, crooked, greedy, money-grubbing—"

"Okay, Bonnie. I get the idea. But what makes people like that? Why does someone turn into a person who appears—at least from what we know of him—to be so in love with money? There are so many other important things in life. Why pick money to be the most important?"

"You know, it probably has something to do with that phony, baloney religion of his. What is New Age, anyway? What a bunch of hogwash. Each person is their own god! Fiddle-faddle!"

Bonnie and Elaine were the last to arrive at Adriana's house. Ramon, Maria, Billy, and Mary were in deep discussion when Adriana opened the front door.

"Come inside. We were going over our progress so far."

Bonnie wasted no time getting down to business. "Well, who is on our side?"

Billy smiled. "Just about everyone. At least, everyone we spoke with today."

"That is good news," Elaine agreed.

Mary added, "Yes, Adriana and I knocked on every door in the old town neighborhood, and then we went to the shops and cafés downtown. Most of the community leaders will be here by 6:30 this evening to finalize our future actions."

Adriana thrust her arms up in the air. "Oh!" We displayed every single flyer about the concert and handed out piles of brochures!"

"It sounds like today was a success," Elaine said. "Now, for the meeting in exactly two hours, let's go over our points for discussion."

"Wait," Bonnie blurted. "You have to tell them."

"Oh, yes. A lot happened on the beach since we met yesterday."

"But that was only a few hours ago," Mary said. "Well?"

Elaine began with the story about Trent on the beach and his questioning Christ and the church. She continued with their meeting with Pastor Sam and his decision to call the executive committee. Her story was interrupted by Adriana's phone ringing.

"Yes, that's correct, 6:30," Adriana replied. She hung up and told the group, "I've been getting calls all day from people wanting to come to the meeting tonight. Sorry."

"Well, for Pete's sakes, how many are going to show up here?" Mary asked.

"Probably more than will fit comfortably into this house," Adriana said.

"Oh, dear," Bonnie said.

"Yes, and everyone we spoke with today? Well, they are all coming for the concert tomorrow night," Billy said.

Ramon smiled. "Elaine, it looks like this plan might just work."

***

Adriana was correct in her assessment of turnout for the meeting. There were people lined up against the walls, on the floor, on every piece of furniture, and spilling out onto the patio. They were all united in their cause. A few people were obviously missing. Adriana's neighbor who had already sold out; Gladys, who was still at work; and of course, Trent Fortune.

Elaine and the others took turns reporting the news about who was called, how many were planning on attending the concert, and the latest talk about the church and the "Save the Ocelots" theme. After two hours, the attendees began to trickle out the door, vowing they would all see the others at the concert the following day.

***

Without a doubt, the turnout of concert-goers was more than they expected. The beach area around the gazebo was jammed. Billy played every song he had written, recorded or not. The crowd went crazy when he played the song that he and Elaine had co-authored. At the request of loud chants to "play it again," he played the entire song twice. He then segued to an introduction of Elaine and asked her to speak for a few minutes.

'Good evening to you all," she said. "As you all know, we have come together in this community many times in the past to help each other. We came back after Jada—"

Applause interrupted her speech, then quieted down.

"And we find ourselves here again, fighting off another storm. This storm threatens to cover and destroy our beautiful little town and seashore. It threatens our tranquility, our peace, and more importantly, our beliefs and our natural wildlife and environment. Some may prefer to sell off their homes and make a quick profit. You and I prefer to keep our town quaint and enrich our wildlife. You and I prefer to keep our churches sacred and our values worthy of passing on to others who come long after we are gone from this planet. I believe we can do this, but we might need legal expertise. This is your chance to help us out. Billy, Ramon, Maria, Bonnie, Adriana, Mary, and I will be taking any donations you can spare. Just put your donations in these colorful, plastic sand buckets. If you came with just your flip-flops and beachwear tonight and would like to donate to the cause tomorrow, we will happily take those donations at the coffee shop tomorrow morning. We will be there from nine until noon. Let's do this. Let's save our churches—and the ocelots! Let's save Sabal Palms!"

Applause was accompanied by whistles and cheers as the crowd raced to empty their pockets and donate rapidly to each of the team members collecting the funds. No question that Elaine and the others would be up late counting the money collected in each plastic bucket.

***

It was after eleven when the group left Elaine's cottage. They had gathered following the concert to count the funds collected. The total was over five thousand dollars to go toward attorney's fees, and Elaine believed the sum would grow larger tomorrow at the coffee shop. Saying their goodbyes, everyone departed and planned to meet at nine a.m.

Closing her door, Elaine saw Bella sitting beside the door with her head tilted and her tail wagging. Bella had the "Let me go out" look.

"Sorry, girl. I forgot. Let's go, but we should be quick."

Elaine looked out over the water. There were millions of stars overhead. Out past the edge of the water toward the island, she saw lightning flashing through billowing clouds.

"Looks like another thunderstorm coming, Bella. Let's make it a short walk tonight."

The next flash of lightning brought the most unusual sight she had ever seen.

"Look at that! Bella, did you see it? It looked like it went all the way to the—"

Elaine's words were halted by a loud boom and a burst of flames.

"Oh, no! Bella, I think it struck a boat or something out there. Let's go inside and call the coast guard."

Chapter Fourteen

Trent enjoyed another full day touring the island and the coastline. He took in the Turtle Rescue Center and the Birding and Wildlife exhibits. He even fed the captive alligators. He had never been much of an environmental enthusiast, but he knew these attractions brought in thousands of tourists each year and thousands of dollars each week. He would capitalize on every single one of these established tourism centers and add some of his own. That alone made his heart beat faster. More money.

He returned to the hotel on the island exhausted yet exhilarated. He showered to remove the remaining sand off his feet and put on his comfortable gym shorts and t-shirt. Plopping down on the sofa, he found the room service menu and looked through the choices.

"Hmmm . . . maybe I should go out and eat on the island tonight."

He changed into another beach outfit—complete with a Hawaiian-print shirt, shorts, and sandals—and went downstairs to summon a taxi.

The concierge greeted Trent immediately. "Mr. Fortune, is there something I can do for you?"

"Yes. I would like to go to the best restaurant on the island."

"I can get you into our premier steak and seafood restaurant. They hold a VIP table for our penthouse guests."

"That would be terrific. Do they have good red snapper and oysters? Isn't that the specialty here?"

He grinned and said, "Yes, sir. One of many specialty items."

The limo was called, and Trent was off once again to see the nightlife of the island.

"Here you are, sir. Liam's."

"Looks interesting. Thanks, Jorge. I will be just an hour or so."

"I will be waiting just outside."

Trent was pleased with the red snapper filet and the side of oysters Rockefeller. He enjoyed every side dish, and the service was the best he had experienced in all his dining on the coast.

"Mr. Fortune, hi. I'm Nicolás, the manager here."

Trent extended his hand. "Nice to meet you, Nicolás."

"Did you find everything to your satisfaction?"

"Yes, it was extraordinary. And your servers, the best."

"Good to hear. Before you leave, I thought you might want to go outside to see the view over the bay back toward the mainland."

"Yes, I would like to see that."

Nicolás walked Trent to the door over the outside deck.

Trent scanned the coastline to get his bearings. "Where exactly are we in relation to the mainland coastline?"

"Directly across, you will see the small town of Sabal Palms, and to the left of that, you will see Port Isabel and the causeway. The causeway is lit up, so you won't miss that."

"Thank you. It is a sight to see. I'm sure the other tourists enjoy this outdoor dining area as well."

"Yes. Some prefer to sit here and watch the sunset."

"Understandable."

The setting sun lowered in the pink and orange sky. The lights across the bay on the mainland illuminated the meandering coastline.

A slight sea breeze gently swayed each palm frond above the dock along the back of the restaurant.

"Thank you, Nicolás. I think I will stay here a couple of minutes."

"Yes, sir. Enjoy."

He gazed across what he knew would be one of his greatest success stories. Sabal Palms would add to his already growing net worth. Something caught his eye near the south end of the Sabal Palms beach toward Port Isabel. From what Trent could tell, it looked as if a large gathering was taking place on that end of the beach. "Wonder what that is all about?" he murmured.

Trent surveyed his field of vision along the edge of the island and the coastline. The causeway appeared to be a lit-up, gradually sloped hill with red threads of cars' taillights strewn atop of the bridge. He turned the other direction to scan the northside of the island. He wasn't able to see the end of the northside and was uncertain how far it stretched. Then he had an idea. *A night flight.*

Trent thanked the manager again as he exited the restaurant and found Jorge parked in the front lot.

"Mr. Fortune, how did you like your dinner?"

"It was excellent. Great recommendation. Say, Jorge, can I ask you to take me over to the private airport on the bay? Think I want to take a little night flight to see the island and the coast at night."

"Certainly, sir. I saw it when I flew into the Brownsville airport. It is quite a sight."

In less than an hour, Trent was in his plane taxiing to the end of the runway. He checked in with the tower and took off. The view was worth the trouble. As he glided back and forth and north and south over the island and the coast, he was mesmerized by the lights, the sparkling water reflecting the shoreline lights, and even the scores of cars going over the causeway. He could not stop studying the lighted coastline on the bay and the lights encircling the island and reflecting in the water. He flew back and forth so many times, he lost count. He tilted slightly and even skirted along the coast, where Mexico intersects with Texas, and over the Boca Chica SpaceX grounds.

"This place is a gold mine," he said to himself. "Once more along the Gulf shore, across the island, then back to the bay."

Turning back north, he noticed rapidly increasing thunderhead clouds gathering. Somewhat disgruntled, he mumbled, "Guess I will have to cut it short."

The lightning came so quickly that Trent never knew it was about to hit his plane. He held as tightly as he could and tried to right the plane. A sharp downdraft of the storm pushed the plane downward rapidly. The interior of the fuselage rattled, and metal pieces loosened. Screws, bolts, and other small pieces of debris flew around the inside. The plane was going down. Before Trent could radio in a call, the downward force pushed his head directly into a piece of sharp metal.

Trent was unconscious when the plane exploded.

***

Darkness. Warmth. Slimy, swimming nudges against his leg. Salt stinging his eyes. Throbbing head. Salt burning his eyes and nose. Tired arms. Holding on to something to stay afloat. *Hold on. Hold on. Don't let go. Hold on. Am I drowning?*

Hold on.

Bobbing. Darkness, darkness. Slimy, swimming things. Squirmy, wriggling under the water. *Hold on. Don't let go. What's happening? Hold on.*

Sleep.

Noise. Planes? Helicopters? Lights streaming across the water.

"Here, over here," he weakly said. "Wait. Here. Over here." *They can't hear me.* He sobbed.

The lights turned away. Searching in the wrong direction.

"Wait. Wait." Trent whispered. He could muster no more strength. He could not yell. He could not wave his arms. Sobbing.

Hold on. Hold on.

Trent was asleep once again.

Wake up. Breathe.

Exhausted, dehydrated, sleepy. His fingers slipped off the floating piece of the plane. He lost his grip. He plunged. Lower. *I'm going to die. I'm drowning.*

Trent shook. *Wake up! Wake up!*

He was flailing and kicking.

Tread water. Tread water.

He dozed once again. He could not stay awake.

Wake up. Wake up.

Gasping for air, he wondered, *Am I going to die?*

His heart was beating too fast. *I'm going to die.*

Tread water. Just tread water.

"Trent, Trent," the Voice said. "Trent."

Slowly turning to the side. A light. A flashlight? *A search light?*

"Hello," Trent mumbled, unable to speak loudly. "Someone there? Hello." *Can't talk loud enough. He can't hear me. Over here. Over here. Help me.* Sobbing. *Help me.*

"Trent. I have called you."

"What?" he murmured.

"Trent, you are Mine. You have been Mine since childhood."

Trent had no idea Who was talking to him.

"What's happening? Hello?"

A Voice pierced the silence. "You will live."

"Who's there?" He gasped.

"Trent, you know Who I am. You have My Spirit. I have called you. *'Fear not, for I have redeemed you; I have called you by name, you are mine.'"*[2]

Squinting, Trent looked toward the sound of the Voice. He saw only a silhouette with light glowing around the entire figure.

"Help me, please, help me," Trent pled.

"You have been saved. *'Be still and know that I am God.'*[3] Live for Me now. You will know what to do. My Spirit is with you."

Trent felt a warmth cover his entire body from head to toe.

Just as suddenly, He disappeared.

With those last words, a large piece of the wing floated up to Trent. He grasped the buoyant wood and held onto it. He cried. Tears began and would not cease. The sobbing was uncontrollable. "Forgive me, please," he pleaded. "Father, forgive me." He shook. He cried and could not stop. And then, the tears continued but turned from sorrow to joy. He was crying with joy.

---

2   Isaiah 43:1
3   Psalm 46:10

He was saved. He would live. He knew Who the Figure was. He knew he would survive.

In the middle of the deep, dark ocean with no help nearby, Trent felt happy. He was relieved. He would live. He knew it now. He knew exactly what had happened. He was almost killed. But then, he was given a second chance, and now he would take it. He would live his life completely differently. A second chance! He smiled. *I didn't die. He saved me. I didn't die. Thank You, Jesus.*

Trent held on to the floating piece of the plane and relaxed. He slept peacefully and was not afraid. He knew he would not die.

***

The sun was up brightly over the water long before Trent woke up. Water as far as he could see. No land in sight. The waves were gentle, and his nausea was gone.

He held on tightly to the small piece of the wing that had kept him afloat through the night. He was sore, exhausted, thirsty, and hungry. He had no idea what the time was or how far out to sea he had floated. He only knew he was alive, and his heart was bursting with gladness.

Trent watched the birds fly overhead. *Brown pelicans.* He knew they were brown pelicans because he had visited the birding center just yesterday. He wondered if it was yesterday. He also knew they were endangered, and he was never so excited to know he was alive another day to see these magnificent birds in flight. He watched the birds dive almost directly straight down, retrieve a fish, and jet back up into the air.

He looked out over the water, straining his eyes to find land. He scanned back and forth. No sign of anything. No land, no boats, nothing as far as he could see.

Trent's lips began to crack. It was ironic that he was out in the middle of water, yet his lips and mouth were parched. His fingers showed signs of wrinkling up from too much water.

The sun rose to midday height, and Trent continued bobbing along just as he had during the night.

He touched his forehead as if to recall the details of what had happened. He recalled vividly the words he had heard from his Savior. But as for the crash, he didn't remember much. A flash of light, something painful to his forehead. He touched it again, then saw the blood on his fingers.

"That's not good," he said.

The sudden rising and gliding motion of the water caught his attention. A dolphin happened by. Not just one, but three.

They swam closer, back and forth, and around.

Do they see me? Are they wanting to be near me?

Watching dolphins in the wild was something he had never done. It was soothing, peaceful. He was completely entertained. These mammals looked as if they were dancing in the water. To his surprise, the dolphins swam nearer and jumped completely out of the water. This routine was repeated time and again. Trent delighted in the performance and almost forgot his predicament.

He wondered if the dolphins knew he was a human who needed help. They stayed with him for what must have been hours. Gliding, swimming around him, jumping in the air, and gracefully submerging again. *These mammals are smart.* They stayed together, and it seemed they were there for a purpose. They did not leave him.

The days and nights passed slowly. The dolphins stayed nearby. Trent was not discouraged. He knew he would be found. He knew he had much work to do. He would sleep until someone happened by. Someone must be looking for him by now. Someone must care that he has disappeared. Then he wondered, *Does anyone care that I am gone? Who would care? Would Shirley care?*

He knew he would live because God had told him he would. He told him to live for Him now. Trent would do just that. He realized, at last, that if he wanted someone to care about him—to care if he was alive or not—he first needed to care about other people. He would start over. He could do it. He knew he could because God told him so Himself. He smiled again.

For days and nights, he watched the dolphins and believed they were watching him.

In the late afternoon of the third day, Trent grew weak and had difficulty holding on to the wing of the plane. One of the dolphins slowly swam near and held Trent steady so he would remain afloat. Trent was tired, hungry, thirsty, and weak, yet happy. The dolphin braced him against the wing.

I'm not going to die.

He slept.

Chapter Fifteen

In an unusual turn of events, at 5:45 a.m., Elaine was awakened by loud banging on her cottage door. Bella mustered up a small bark to announce that her tiny stature would somehow be able to protect Elaine.

With her bathrobe halfway on, Elaine cautiously opened the front door. Before her stood Bonnie, already dressed for their morning walk.

"What on earth? Bonnie, are you okay?"

"I am, but not so sure about those poor people."

"What poor people?"

"I heard on the local news that a plane was struck by lightning last night. It was just offshore."

"That's what that was? I was outside and heard it. I called the coast guard. I thought it struck a ship, and the ship exploded. Come in."

Bonnie followed Elaine inside and continued her conversation. "I turned on the local news like I always do in the morning when I am testing my blood sugar; that's when I saw the story. For heaven's sakes, can you imagine?"

Elaine staggered toward the coffee pot and scooped coffee into the basket. "Coffee?"

"Please."

Elaine filled the pot with water. "Those unfortunate people. Any other details?"

Bonnie nodded. "Just that the search was discontinued because of the storm and darkness. They're going to start back again today. The coast guard official said they feared the type of explosion and the choppy water may now turn the mission from one of rescue to recovery. They said the chances were next-to-impossible that anyone would survive such an explosion. The longer the time to find them, the graver it would be."

"That is horrible. Just awful. I will keep their families and, hopefully, the survivors in my prayers," Elaine said.

Elaine and Bonnie each had their coffee, and Elaine put a light breakfast together.

"Good thing you came over so early. We have to be at the coffee shop before nine."

"Do we have time for a quick walk?"

"I think so."

Elaine fed Bella, and she and Bonnie finished their breakfast. Elaine threw on her walking shorts.

"Let's go. Come on, Bella," Elaine called.

Along the sand, Bonnie stopped. "Think we can see anything out there? Like wreckage?"

Elaine stopped and looked intently. "I see a couple of boats. Probably shrimpers going out."

"Or coast guard." Bonnie shook her head. "Just awful. I wonder if the pilot knew the weather was going to turn bad?"

"It seemed to come on pretty quickly when I was walking Bella."

They chatted about the concert, the turnout, and their plans for the day on their short morning walk.

"I'll pick you up in about thirty minutes," Elaine announced.

"I'll be ready."

***

Soon, the women departed for the short journey into the small downtown area of Sabal Palms.

The turn out onto the highway brought an unusual sight. "Will you look at that! I've never seen that kind of a truck before. What do you suppose that guy is going to do?" Bonnie asked.

"I've never seen that either. I've seen cranes, but never one that big. It is headed toward the water. And there is another truck behind it."

"And a couple of cars," Bonnie noted.

The large piece of equipment was an enormous crane. Following the crane was another large flatbed truck and two vehicles.

"Elaine, do you suppose it has something to do with the plane going down last night?"

"Possibly."

Driving along the palm tree-lined road, Elaine noticed three parked cars in front of a rebuilt house.

"There are the lucky buyers," Bonnie said. "Got themselves a deal, I'm sure. Those new, nosy people from who-knows-where. So many people selling. And then this Trent fellow coming in to buy so much of the land around Sabal Palms. And poor Adriana having to worry about her neighbor selling and Trent wanting to buy part of her land."

"I think our actions will go a long way in helping the town to fight this guy. We already raised a good bit of the needed funds for hiring an attorney."

"True. And today, even more will come in. Did you bring the money from last night so we can total it after our collections this morning?" Bonnie asked.

"Yes. I put all the money in an overnight bag in the trunk of the car. And this morning, while we wait for more funds, we will be sipping delicious, fresh-roasted coffee!"

"Goodness," Elaine said. "Look at all the cars. I guess we will have to park a few blocks away. Lots of people downtown early today."

Elaine parked the car a few blocks away. Mary parked behind Elaine and Bonnie.

"Good morning, girls."

"Hi, Mary," Elaine replied. "Are you ready for this?"

Soon, Billy, Adriana, Ramon, and Maria trickled in shortly after Bonnie, Elaine, and Mary. In file, they walked up the street several blocks, where they discovered a line of local residents waiting at the front door of the coffee shop.

Juan and Cara motioned to Elaine to come to the front of the line. "Come on up. We are waiting for you. We already ordered our coffees."

"Oh, my goodness!" Elaine exclaimed. "Look at this! So many people."

A spontaneous chant began from the line. "Save Sabal Palms! Save Sabal Palms!"

Bonnie and Mary, both nearly in a tizzy with excitement, began a string of exclamations. Bonnie started with "Impressive!"

Mary added, "Magnificent!"

"Fantastic!"

"Splendid!"

"Momentous!"

Finally, Billy interrupted their silliness and asked, "Ladies, you are so good with words, want to write my next song?"

They laughed and stepped inside the door of the coffee shop.

***

The group pulled three tables together so they would all be available to speak with individuals, collect money, and answer any questions. The group of seven had sand buckets on the table for collection. Elaine was amazed by the turnout of people. The residents came by their tables to donate money to the cause. She guessed that by noon, they would collect as much as they had the night before at the concert. Maybe even more.

In addition to the concert and Trent Fortune's development plans, the talk of the morning was the plane crash.

Myrtle Witherspoon was among the first to bring up the subject. "I was absolutely stunned when I heard the news. The storm didn't reach our house last night, so I had no idea. I just couldn't believe it."

Elaine replied, "It looked like the storm was out to sea a bit—at least the worst of it. I didn't stay outside after the lightning struck. I went in and called the coast guard."

Myrtle continued, "It must have been out there a ways. I hope those poor folks are found. I have been praying for them."

"I prayed many times since I heard the news," Elaine said.

"Prayer is a powerful thing. It is the best thing, and the only thing we can do."

"You're right, Myrtle."

Martha Lewis wheeled up to the table next. "Hi, Elaine, Bonnie, and all of you. I just wanted to personally thank you for what you are doing. I know we can beat this thing."

Bonnie said, "I agree, Martha! I think we have *this* particular bull by the horns!"

A look of concern came upon Martha's face. "I heard the news about that plane last night. Just awful. I am guessing it was probably tourists."

Elaine added, "That would make sense. Maybe one of those tourist charters or something."

"I've been praying for those people all night long and this morning," Martha said.

"Prayer *is* powerful," Elaine confirmed.

Martha was soon followed by Cara.

"Cara," Elaine said, "I haven't seen you in a while."

Cara laughed. "Not since last Sunday! Gladys told me about the plans this developer has for the church. I had to come by. I don't have much money, working part-time and everything, but I wanted to give something to the cause."

"You are a blessing," Elaine said.

"And, Elaine," she said with a quivering lip, "I haven't forgotten what you did for me last year."

Elaine rose from the table and hugged Cara. "That wasn't me, sweetie," she whispered. "That was Jesus."

Cara hugged her again. "Thank you. I know you played a part, Elaine."

Elaine hugged Cara tightly.

The morning continued with the kind words, prayers, and donations from the townspeople. Last to stop by, precisely at noon, was the mayor, Richard Townsend. Elaine's stomach knotted up a bit when he entered the coffee shop. He approached the table.

"Elaine, I'm not sure what you are doing is a good idea. The town . . . well, the town needs the revenue that this development will bring."

"Yes, sir. I understand that. I'm just not sure this development is the best way to generate the revenue."

"I would be happy to entertain any other ideas to generate revenue you might have. But, Elaine, just so you are aware, this fellow, Trent Fortune, has a lot of resources to bring. He will use them all to get this thing done. I know how he works. He has quite a successful track record. I don't think all the donations in the world are going to be enough to stop him."

"I will keep that in mind, sir. But you must know, Mayor Townsend, that we will bring all our resources as well. We happened to have a Resource with much more power." She looked upward and pointed to the ceiling.

Mayor Townsend laughed. "I know, Elaine, I know."

***

After the crowd dwindled down and the donations stopped pouring in, the working group of seven collected their buckets and agreed to gather at Mary's house to count the funds.

Mary arrived at her home first and unlocked the front door. Billy brought the money in from Elaine's trunk, and everyone else brought in plastic buckets, stuffed with money, collected at the coffee shop from their own cars.

Mary scurried around her kitchen assembling a smorgasbord of healthy salads and cold slices of turkey and ham. The hungry team filled their plates and sat down around the breakfast table and the counter.

"Have tea and lemonade over here, and in case you didn't get enough coffee this morning, I put on a fresh pot for this afternoon."

The munching noises were nonstop, along with the "oohs" and "ahs" uttered around the room.

Billy visited the counter buffet for seconds. "Mary, as usual, outstanding."

"Thank you. Just want to be sure you all keep coming back over," she said and laughed.

"No worries about that," Bonnie assured her. "You keep feeding us, we'll show up."

Elaine smiled. "Mary, we all enjoy your company, not just the food."

Once lunch was consumed, the counting began.

"Elaine," Ramon said, "you were correct. We topped last night's pot. We collected a little over six thousand dollars today."

"You know, since we collected more than five thousand last night, I think our grand total will be close to twelve thousand dollars."

Adriana, who had been nearly silent all morning, began waving her arms and jangling her bracelets with excitement. "Twelve thousand! That is . . . my stars! Twelve thousand?"

"Yes!" Bonnie exclaimed. "We will show that . . . that scoundrel! He can't mess with Sabal Palms!" Bonnie kiddingly held her two fists in the air.

Laughter filled the kitchen, and for at least a few moments, the group laughed and talked together like the close friends they were.

Everyone in the group agreed it had been a busy couple of days.

"How about if we all take the rest of the day off and just relax," Mary suggested.

"That would be grand. Now, if anyone wants to jump in my pool this afternoon, I will be happy to have you," Adriana said.

"I'm with Mary," Elaine said. "I think I will take the rest of the day off. Church might be interesting in the morning."

"That's right," Bonnie said. "Maybe Pastor Sam will have some news. It is his last Sunday, after all."

***

On the way home, Elaine and Bonnie agreed to take a short walk on the beach.

"Well, you know I have to keep my blasted blood sugar down. More walking."

Elaine laughed. "It's good for me, also. And the vet told me at Bella's last checkup that she is a pound heavy for her size! I have to put her on a diet!"

"Oh, horsefeathers! A diet for a dog! A bunch of malarkey, if you ask me."

"Of course, walking is good for her, too."

Elaine and Bella made it down to Bonnie's cottage quickly.

"Can you believe it?" Bonnie asked. "Nearly twelve thousand dollars?"

"That's a great start!"

"Want to walk north for a change? Up to the more desolate part of the beach?" Bonnie asked.

"Sounds good." They turned back north and walked. "Come on, Bella, going this way now."

The calming breeze and sound of the waves was exactly what Elaine needed. She had been tense the last few days, and her research about the goings-on with Trent Fortune left little time for writing and reading her Bible. She was always better, more centered, and more relaxed when she made time for that.

The threesome walked for over a mile up the shore. And that is when they saw it.

"For heaven's sakes!" Bonnie said.

"Will you look at that!" Elaine said.

Bella barked and ran frantically back and forth, not sure what the large things on the beach were and if they would be a threat.

Before their eyes, probably two hundred yards away, the giant crane pulled up what looked like the fuselage of a small plane. Two men were in the water, assisting.

"I'm totally flabbergasted!" Bonnie said.

Elaine could not believe what was before her. "The plane crash," she mumbled.

Bonnie pointed further up the beach. "That truck! It is loaded with junk, like other pieces of the wreckage."

"But no word yet of who it was or any survivors. So sad. Pray for them, Bonnie. That's all we can do to help."

***

"Come in; come in!" Pastor Sam greeted the entering congregants as they passed through the little church's front doors.

Elaine and Bonnie sat near the front. Mary came in next, followed by Adriana, whose perfume preceded her and found its way to the front of the sanctuary long before she did.

The women scooted down to make room for Billy, Ramon, and Maria, who followed Adriana. Nods and hellos were quietly exchanged.

Pastor Sam led the service with the typical announcements about Bible study class and the prayer list for those who had requested a special prayer by the congregation. At the end of the extended prayer list, Pastor Sam paused. "Now, this morning, I am asking you all to join me in special prayer for the person, or people, who were flying around the island when a sudden storm ended the flight. We know pieces of the plane have been recovered. We will all pray that the mission is still one of rescue rather than recovery. And should the mission end up being only for recovery, we pray for the families and loved ones of these individuals."

Following the prayers and hymns, Pastor Sam began a sermon with the topic of change. He mentioned, as everyone already knew, he had received a call for another church. He then began a discussion of various verses about change. Among the ones he brought out were some of Elaine's favorites.

In reassuring the congregation that they would survive any change of leadership or of pastors, he discussed Hebrews 13:8: "Jesus Christ is the same yesterday and today and forever."

He then talked about the changes coming to Sabal Palms and told the congregation to be inspired by Scripture. He reminded the people of Deuteronomy 31:6: "'Be strong and courageous. Do not fear or be in dread of them, for it is the LORD your God who goes with you. He will not leave you or forsake you.'"

And another Old Testament verse he felt was very important to remember in the days ahead if they were exposed to false prophecies was Malachi 3:6: "'For I the LORD do not change; therefore you, O children of Jacob, are not consumed.'"

Pastor Sam said, "Be strong. You stand your ground and be firm in your beliefs. I would like to tell you all, the executive committee will be meeting following the service. They will be extending another invitation for applications for a new pastor. The search process will continue until a suitable candidate, one who affirms his belief in Christ, is invited for an interview. The candidate will be required to undergo an extensive background reference check, and he will be required to preach at least for one Sunday and receive favorable reviews by the congregation."

With his last words, applause broke out so loudly, Elaine was certain the stained-glass windows rattled. The crowd cheered, and smiles broke out across the church in every pew. Mary leaned over and whispered, "Goodbye, Cousin Kathy and Charles."

Chapter Sixteen

It was just a matter of time before Trent Fortune's investors were told that Trent's plane went missing. The group, based in Florida, agreed to meet to determine what to do next. The permits and formal proposal for the development of Sabal Palms had not yet been submitted to the town or county officials. In discussion with the town mayor, they learned there was an undercurrent movement among the townspeople to stop the development project. However, the investors, like Trent, were greedy and looking to make easy money. What's more, they believed in the mission Trent had outlined, which included repurposing the little church for the promotion of New Age religion.

Mr. Franklin led the charge. He called Trent's office and requested the group use the conference room and that the assistant, Shirley, attend and bring all records and up-to-date documents for review. Shirley agreed.

Shirley had worked with Trent for fifteen years, since he had opened the first small Florida office. His increasing net worth meant he had, over the years, moved into larger offices, each one with a better view and more square footage. His company now amassed an army of worker bees. But none of those minions had achieved what Shirley had. While she initially admired Trent's instincts of finding opportunistic ways to increase his net worth, she had hoped all these years that she, too, would reap the rewards. Trent kept her at his side and increased her salary along the way. She was loyal to a fault and passed up many offers from other wealthy investors to leave Trent and join their companies. None of those older, rounder, and rougher men were as handsome as Trent. That was another disappointment for Shirley many years ago. She had tried to kindle that fire. But Trent insisted on keeping their relationship professional. In fact, he never had time for women or any social life as far as she could tell. Cocktail parties, dinners, and any event on his calendar were strictly goal-oriented. Always seeking more ways to connect with people to make money. But now that Trent was gone, this was *her* chance, and she would take it.

***

Shirley greeted the investors, who took their seats around the conference table. "Gentlemen, please come in. As you know, the coast guard is searching fervently for Trent. It is my understanding that several pieces of the plane have been pulled from the Gulf of Mexico near Padre Island. In the meantime, progress should move forward on this venture.

"I took the liberty of ordering a lunch for each of you according to your preferences expressed to me by your assistants. It will be here shortly." The men smiled at Shirley's attentiveness to detail.

"I have placed new binders for each of you around the table with the updated information and reports Trent filed just last week. I updated the presentation, and if you turn to the screen, we will begin there."

A knock on the conference room door announced the arrival of an exquisite lunch, delectable in every way. The server placed each plate, complete with the name of each investor inscribed on individual place cards, before each investor.

Shirley could read body language well. It was something on which she prided herself. She could read the room and make the difference for Trent at any cocktail party. She told him exactly what each person in the room thought about his comments, and she suggested how he should handle it. She wondered what Trent would have done without her all those years.

Shirley observed the delight of each attendee as the server lifted the silver cover of each dish. Their expressions of curiosity changed to joy when each one distinguished that their lunch was their favorite food.

She glanced around the table. Mr. Franklin smiled as he took bites of his lunch and turned the pages. Mr. Green nodded and said, "Yes, yes," under his breath and dug into another bite. Dinero looked pleasantly surprised turning the pages and cutting his perfectly cooked steak.

Even with these positive reactions about their lunches, nothing could top the reaction they each had to Shirley's business investment proposal. She began with the financials and displayed the differences between her newest concepts for allocations of investments and where the money would bring the greatest returns. Her estimates were much higher than Trent's because she maneuvered the funds around according to the most recent revenues using online public data from the South Padre Island Chamber of Commerce and their local bankers and investors groups.

Dinero was the first to comment. "These figures—this revised proposal is remarkable. Did Trent send you this before he went missing?"

"Gentlemen, these are my own estimates. You see, I have learned from the best. Being involved in Trent's projects over the years and following his pattern of investing, I have been able to skillfully apply each aspect of his investment strategy. And while we all hope he will be found, in the worst-case scenario, I would like to stay onboard with this project for the duration."

Franklin replied, "That would be—"

She interrupted, "For twenty-five percent of the net profit."

The room was silent, but not for long.

"Gentlemen, indeed, she *has* learned from the best." Dinero laughed. "I would like to say—assuming this would be approved by Trent if he is found—that I believe the addition of Shirley to this particular endeavor would be an excellent idea. She has done her homework and has improved our projected earnings in a significant way."

Franklin said, "I agree. Perhaps, however, we should also discuss a contingency if Trent is located."

Shirley didn't want this to go haywire. She volunteered, "But of course, should we be fortunate enough to locate Trent, we can renegotiate. That said, I would like to remain a partner at some level."

Green said, "It sounds reasonable to me."

Franklin suggested, "And should he be found, we might renegotiate so that we each earn an equal amount of the net, which would be twenty percent."

Shirley jotted down a few notes and agreed without showing her emotions. She smiled internally. *Worked exactly as I planned.*

***

In the southern part of the Gulf of Mexico a few miles off South Padre Island, Trent Fortune floated aimlessly. Between the stormy seas the night before, the scorching sun, and the high waves, he was miserably tossed about and drifted further than the coast guard anticipated in their initial search. He was now between a state of consciousness and unconsciousness. He felt he was in some type of altered state. But when he was able to think, he remembered the Voice. He remembered the lighted Silhouette. He remembered the words: "You know Me; you have My Spirit. I have called you. *'Fear not, for I have redeemed you; I have called you by name, you are mine.'*"[4]

Sleep. Bobbing. Heat. Such heat.

He prayed. "Father, I know You will save me. I have faith, and I thank You."

Sleep. Burning sun.

The dolphins returned once again.

There you are.

Trent had no idea of the time or day. Had he been missing one day? Two? Three?

Sleep.

The dolphin braced against him once again.

Father, please. Your will is mine. Father . . .

Blistering sun. Sleep. Unconsciousness.

Tossing. Dolphin nudged again.

Thank you, my friend.

Unconsciousness.

***

---

4   Isaiah 43:1

He wasn't certain how, but he was transported in time and space. At least in his mind. Trent was in his old home. He was four years of age, and his grandmother had picked him up early for church. He was excited because he wasn't going to go to church with his father this Sunday. His grandmother expressly asked to take the youngster to her church to meet her church friends.

"Come, sweetheart," his grandmother said. "Today, we are going to have such fun."

Trent smiled. She always made him feel special. She never hit him. Even after church. She didn't yell or slap anyone.

Grandma? How could she be here with me? Is Grandma with me?

He climbed into her old car, and she started up the engine. They rattled down a small, country road toward the old, country church.

"Now, our only decision today is if we want to have fried chicken or barbecue after church. The ladies are bringing both. And, oh my! There will be such desserts! They will have chocolate pie." She smiled.

"My favorite!" Trent said.

"Now, today, church will be a little different. Today, the pastor is going to ask you a very important question."

"He is?"

"Yes, dear. He will talk to you about Jesus and ask if He is in your heart."

"Is He in there?"

"Yes, if you accept Him as your Savior. He is in the hearts of all children who believe in Him. You just must know it and feel He is in there and let Him stay in your heart forever. Then, when you are a little older, you will learn more about it."

"I will?"

"Yes. You will learn all the Bible stories. Your mother and father agreed I could take you to church *every* week from now on."

"Really? And eat dessert?"

She laughed. "Yes, dear. And eat dessert."

Trent was there at the old church again. He recalled the teacher walking all the preschool children to the front of the church. He recalled the pastor's words. He felt that warmth in his heart. He felt Jesus there just at the moment the pastor asked him, "Do you have Jesus in your heart?"

Trent nodded. "Yes. He is in here." He pointed to his heart.

"And He will always be there," the pastor said.

Grandma? Am I with you? Am I dead?

"No, my child. You won't see me for many years," she replied. "You have much work to do first."

His grandmother's sudden death from a heart attack six months after that Sunday ended the weekly Sunday school and church days. That was when he was forced to go back to church with his own parents. That was when his father beat him again on Sundays. And other days. And that was when he hated church.

***

Trent smiled thinking of his grandmother. He hadn't thought of her in a long time. Would he see her soon?

I am not going to die.

He smiled. *Jesus. In my heart. I am not going to die. He saved me.*

The dolphin nudged his leg.

Heat. Blisters on his mouth.

Bobbing. Sun. Waves.

Thank you, sweet animal.
Bobbing. Heat. Sun.

***

Trent was unaware that he was in and out of consciousness. He didn't hear the helicopter blades whirring high above his head. He didn't feel his lifeless body being lifted off the piece of the wing by the coast guard. He didn't know ropes of a basket were placed around his limp torso and hooked to the rope to pull him up. He didn't even notice when the basket lifted into the sky.

For a second, his eyes opened. *I'm flying to Heaven.*

He vaguely heard a voice.

"An unidentified male. Possibly the missing pilot, Trent Fortune. No. He is unconscious. Small breaths. No. Faint heartbeat. Yes. Coming your way. ID? We'll check." Trent did not notice when the coast guard rescue team took his wallet from his pocket. "Yes. Confirmed. Trent Fortune."

***

Lights. Bright. Noise. Moving.

"Mr. Fortune. Trent. Can you hear me?"

Unconscious.

His arms and legs were moved around. He felt his body being lifted onto something hard. It was a cart or table or board of some kind. Rolling. Bumping on concrete.

"Mr. Fortune."

Eyes pried open.

Bright light.

Stop. Stop the light.

"Mr. Fortune. Trent. Can you hear me?"

Silence. Moving. Rolling.

Eyes opened briefly.

Hallway? Where? Not my office.

"Trent?"

"Okay, let's lift him. One, two, three."

Bed.

"Mr. Fortune. I'm Dr. Salazar. Can you hear me? You were rescued from the water. Do you know where you are? Trent?"

Unconscious.

Beep. Beep. Beep. Beep.

Sleep.

***

Shirley's phone buzzed.

"Hello. What? What? Oh my! That's amazing. Yes. How is he? What hospital? Brownsville? Yes. I will take a flight today. Is he . . . is he okay? Broken ribs? I see . . . scrapes and bruises. Weak but stable? Yes. Of course."

With no spouse and no contact with his parents, Trent had always listed Shirley as the person to call in case of emergency. Now, she was tasked with the duty of calling the investors. At least, she'd had enough time and good sense to grab the opportunity of getting her seat at the investor table. She was assured of her spot because she had prepared in advance the documents for the investors to sign, which she had notarized the same day. She had amended the agreement with the twenty-percent division should Trent be found alive.

For a moment, she wondered if Trent would be mad at her for edging her way in. Maybe she should have asked him years ago to become an investor. He certainly should know her value and worth after the years of dedication to his every whim. She held that office together. She had been the glue. She had saved him from near mistakes. Mistakes that would have been costly. He must have appreciated that, although he never told her.

She contacted the airline and booked a first-class ticket for later that afternoon into Harlingen. She arranged for a limo to pick her up and take her to the hospital.

She packed a small bag, then sent for Trent's limo. She would be able to call the investors on the way to the airport. They would be relieved. And she was secure in her position on the venture.

***

Throughout the day, Trent was poked, probed, examined. He was not aware.

He was hooked up to IVs for fluids and provided with oxygen. His heart was monitored continuously. His head wound was cleaned and dressed. He was unconscious and didn't notice any of it.

"Heart looks to be improving," a nurse announced to Dr. Salazar, who entered the room.

"That's good news. How he survived this, God only knows. He beat the odds. A plane crash and explosion, lost at sea for three days. Unbelievable."

"He definitely was given a second chance," the nurse agreed. "The coast guard said he was kept afloat by a group of dolphins."

"Dolphins? That's a great story."

"They said he was floating partially on a piece of the airplane wing; and the dolphins supported his leg, helped to keep him afloat, and protected him."

"Got to love a good dolphin story. You're right. He was given a second chance."

"Divine intervention. Isn't that what they say?"

"Yes."

Second chance. I'm alive.

"Mr. Fortune. Trent?" Dr. Salazar said. "I thought I saw a bit of responsiveness. Next of kin called? Is someone coming?"

"Yes. No family but someone from work. His emergency contact."

"When are they expected?"

"Tonight, I believe."

"Good. Keep pushing fluids and watch him for any other symptoms of shock. I'm on call today. Keep me updated, say at least every hour or so."

"Will do."

Silence. Dry. Not bobbing. Still. Quiet. Sleep.

Beep. Beep. Beep. Beep.

Eyes. Can't open.

Turn over! Turn. Things in arms. Needles? *Where am I?*

"Mr. Fortune," the nurse said. She touched his leg. "Can you hear me? Are you with me?"

He moved slightly. He felt the ache in his side. He took painful breaths.

"That's wonderful, Mr. Fortune. Can you hear me?"

Trying as hard as he possibly could, he managed to open his eyes slightly.

"Mr. Fortune. There you are. I will let the doctor know . . . "

Trent opened his mouth and attempted to speak.

"Yes?" the nurse leaned over. "Did you want to tell me something?"

He tried to nod.

"Yes?"

He uttered only two words. "Elaine Smith."

"What's that?" The nurse leaned closer to Trent.

He whispered, "Elaine Smith. Sabal Palms."

"Do you want me to contact her?"

He nodded and closed his eyes.

Chapter Seventeen

Elaine dressed and had thirty minutes before she would pick Bonnie up, drive to Adriana's, and plan the petition for the commissioner's meeting. The group decided to meet in time for lunch and spend the afternoon preparing the documents they would need for the next step in the process of stopping the development.

"Time to read," she told Bella. She grabbed her Bible and sat in her cozy chair by the window overlooking the shore. For most of her life, Elaine followed a standard plan to read the Bible in one year. But lately, she opened the Bible to a random page and began to read. She felt that God would assist her by letting the Bible fall open at the exact point. It never mattered what page she found; she learned something every single time.

The page opened. Matthew 18:12-14. "What do you think? If a man has a hundred sheep, and one of them has gone astray, does he not leave the ninety-nine on the mountains and go in search of the one that went astray? And if he finds it, truly, I say to you, he rejoices over it more than over the ninety-nine that never went astray. So it is not the will of my Father who is in heaven that one of these little ones should perish."

"Leave the ninety-nine," she whispered. Elaine stared out the window wondering what the meaning was for her today. *Maybe this means Jesus will find someone who is lost today. Maybe He will help me find someone. A lost sheep.* She read the passage over and over. She said another prayer for the people who were in the plane crash, then placed the Bible on the table.

"Okay, Bella, gotta run. You be a good girl." She patted Bella on the head, and the pooch wagged her short stub of a tail and walked Elaine to the door.

***

Bonnie climbed in Elaine's car and slammed the door.

"Are you okay?"

"Yes. Just that the more I think about this scoundrel, the angrier I feel. Scallywag. Swindler."

"Bonnie, you shouldn't let Trent and his development eat you up. We have a great plan in place. Today is just the beginning."

"And exactly what are we supposed to accomplish today?"

"Today, we're meeting to draw up the petition to the commissioners."

"And?"

"Then, the petition asks the commissioners to appoint a zoning committee to study our request about the property. Then, we hope they will accept our appeal—assuming Trent has already applied to the zoning committee for changing his purchased property to commercial zoning."

"Oh, gobbledygook! Sounds like we are just jumping through one hoop after another."

"You know, Bonnie, that's exactly what we are doing, hoop-jumping. But there is no quick way to do this, and we have to follow the process."

"Ugh. All just a brouhaha!"

"Maybe. But it is all we can do—other than pray, of course."

"Elaine, what about the attorney? When do we get the attorney involved?"

"Good question, and we should find out today. Billy texted he will be a little late this morning because he is contacting a few of his friends first. Once he gets some recommendations, we can call them."

Adriana stood on the porch beckoning each of her guests to come inside. "Girls, come on in. And Ramon, oh! Look! You brought tomatoes! And peppers!"

Ramon and Maria shared each new batch of their vegetables with the entire gang. In exchange, Bonnie and Mary would trade a pie, cake, or other dessert. Elaine invited them over for dinners and cookouts in which she served the garden-fresh goodies. And Adriana invited them to use her pool whenever they wanted. Ever since Hurricane Jada, this group stuck together. If anyone needed anything, it was just a phone call away.

Inside, the group settled down to the task at hand. Elaine used Adriana's computer and typed the petition forms. A copy for each of the team members was printed and handed around.

"Okay, let's proof this and see if we want to make any changes or if there are any typos," Elaine directed.

Billy texted Elaine.

"Oh, Billy is on his way. He said he has news," Elaine said. "Now, first, any errors? Additions?"

"Looks fine to me," Mary said.

"Yep. Looks like it covers all the bases," Ramon said.

All agreed.

"Oh, Billy's here!" Adriana bounded off her chair and walked to the front door with jewelry clanging all the way.

"Billy, do come in," she said.

"Adriana," he said as he removed his hat.

Mary blurted out, "What's the news? Do tell! Did you run into Gladys at the store?"

"Hi, no, nothing like that. I just heard it on the radio before I left my apartment. They found the pilot from the plan that crashed the other night in the Gulf. He was taken to the hospital in Brownsville."

Unable to control the waving of her arms, Adriana asked, "What? He's alive? He survived?"

"Who is it?" Bonnie asked.

"All I heard was that they are notifying the family. I suppose they will announce it later. But they did say there only appeared to be the one person in the plane."

"The important thing is that this person is alive," Elaine said.

Curious, Maria asked, "Is he expected to live?"

Ramon added, "Did they say what condition he is in?"

"No, only that he had survived. Nothing more. Now, what kind of progress have you made here?"

Elaine handed Billy a copy of the petition to read.

"Well, while he is reading, I am happy to announce that Mary and I have a few dishes ready for lunch," Adriana said. She opened the overstuffed refrigerator, and Mary assisted with placement on the counter and breakfast table.

Lunch assembly was interrupted by the doorbell.

"My stars, who could that be?" Adriana said. She walked to her door, followed by Mary and Bonnie, while the others remained in the kitchen in the process of getting lunch set out for the group.

"Hello, Deputy Gonzales," Adriana said. "What can I do for you?"

"Sorry to disturb you ladies. But I am looking for Elaine. I went out to her house, and she wasn't there. Thought I would try Mary's and your house. I see her car is here."

"Yes, sir. She's here. Come inside."

Deputy Gonzales, Mary, Adriana, and Bonnie walked back to the kitchen.

"Hello, Elaine, and all." He tipped his hat. "I hate to bother you, but, Elaine, there is someone at the hospital who asked us to contact you."

Puzzled, Elaine replied, "Oh?"

"Yes. I think you know him. Trent Fortune?"

"What? Trent Fortune?"

"Yes. The hospital staff sent for someone back in Florida, but he said he only wants to see you."

"Me? I hardly know him."

"I don't ask questions, Elaine. I just do what I'm told. I was told to come and notify you. Now, you don't have to go. But you can ride with me, or—"

"No, no, I'll go. I'll take my car. Bonnie, uh, Mary, everyone, I will go over to Brownsville to see what is going on. If you don't mind, would someone take Bonnie home after a while?"

"No problem," Mary said. "I'd be happy to."

***

Driving to Brownsville took forty minutes. In that entire amount of time, Elaine could not think of one single reason why a man, presumably not in very good shape, would ask to speak to her. In her mind, she believed that Trent Fortune represented the enemy. She had organized the troops of Sabal Palms to rally around and fight off this beast. She not only was against his development plans to take over much of the quaint town of Sabal Palms, but she also felt in her heart that he was against her own faith, against Christianity, and worse, wanted to bring an evil, false religion to her town. He wanted to destroy the tiny church on the shore and convert it to who-knows-what and possibly change the seaside environment.

Elaine visualized her small stretch of the Texas coastline. It wasn't much, but it was pristine. She wanted to keep it that way. Living there for more than twenty years, she couldn't imagine the changes that might take place. She would no longer be able to sit on her deck in private. There would be noise, loud music, and beachside parties. Not her peaceful beach for quiet walks and dinners on her deck.

***

Elaine approached the receptionist. "Excuse me, can you tell me where to find Trent Fortune?"

"Yes, let me check." The woman searched the files on her computer. "He's on the fourth floor in the intensive care wing. Check in with the nurse's station there."

"Thank you." *Intensive care. He must be in bad shape. Why me?*

Elaine checked in as instructed and told the head nurse her name.

"Yes, Trent asked for you. He can only have one visitor at a time. He is in 409, just to the left."

Elaine slowly opened the door and peeked in. Before her was a pale, weak man with tubes and wires connected in various places. The steady, slow beeps of the heart monitor were the only sounds she heard. She quietly sat in the chair beside the bed.

Trent slept. He didn't move; he didn't talk.

After several minutes, a nurse came in, checked several readings, and changed an IV bag. Trent slept. The nurse left and reappeared an hour later. This routine was repeated all afternoon.

Another nurse pushed the door open. "Mr. Fortune, I have a little something for you to eat. Let's just take it slow and see if you want to taste these." She sat the tray down and looked at Elaine.

"Can you help him if he wakes?"

"Of course."

Trent moved slightly and continued sleeping.

Opening the door thirty minutes later, the nurse said, "He didn't eat anything?"

"No, he has been asleep."

"Mr. Fortune, let's try some applesauce. Just a bite?"

Trent groaned and moved his leg.

"Well, I guess I will take the tray. But I will leave the drinks in case he wants some."

"Okay," said Elaine.

The sunlight from the narrow window began to fade. Elaine adjusted the chair to a reclined position and shut her eyes. Just a brief nap. That was all she wanted.

The door opened again, and the nurse checked the monitors and left.

Trent groaned and opened his eyes. "Elaine. You came."

She sat up in the chair and leaned toward the bed. "Yes, hello."

"Elaine," he said in a soft tone, and Elaine had difficulty hearing him. "Yes?"

"I'm sorry."

"I don't understand."

"I'm sorry. I want to tell you. He came to me."

"Who? I don't understand."

"Elaine, I almost drowned. I almost died. He saved me."

Elaine listened without speaking.

"It was dark, except around Him. Jesus had a glow all around. He was in the dark. Over the water."

"Oh?"

He coughed.

"Are you okay? Can I get you something?"

"No. I'm fine. I have a second chance, Elaine."

"You certainly do. We all thought the people in the plane . . . Well, we wondered if they survived."

"I don't know how long I was out there. There were dolphins. Dolphins helped me. And He was there."

Elaine wondered if he was making any sense. She wondered if perhaps he had been dreaming. She wondered if everything was just his imagination.

"He told me I was His. He came for me."

Trent closed his eyes and slept.

***

Shirley's limo drove her directly to the hospital from the airport. She took her small overnight bag with her to the hospital lobby. Following the receptionist's instructions, she went up to the fourth floor.

"Excuse me, miss, can you tell me where I can find Trent Fortune?"

"And you are?"

"I am Shirley Matthews, his personal assistant."

"I see. He is in intensive care and can only have one visitor at a time."

"Okay, well, it's just me."

"Yes, but he already has a visitor. He only asked to see one person, Elaine Smith, and she is inside."

"Oh?"

"I can check to see if he would like to see you during regular visitor hours tomorrow afternoon."

"Oh, uh, okay."

The nurse walked down the hall and into Trent's room. She returned quickly.

"I'm sorry. He requested no other visitors until he is moved into a regular room."

"And when will that be?"

"The doctor hasn't been by since earlier this afternoon, so I'm not sure. You can call back later and ask."

Frustrated, Shirley huffed and turned to the elevator.

***

Elaine's neck was stiff. She felt sore all over. The clanging of the cart as the door opened startled her.

"Good morning," a too-chirpy nurse announced. "I brought you something to eat for breakfast. Let's give it a try."

The words Trent had said last night played in her mind again. She thought maybe he had been dreaming or was unconscious. Maybe he had hallucinated. She wondered if she would be able to tell the difference. Would he know the difference between reality and a hallucination? She would try when he woke up.

"Mr. Fortune," the nurse repeated.

"Huh?" he answered.

"Try something here? Applesauce? Pudding? A little bite of scrambled eggs?"

"Oh." He sat up.

Trent looked at Elaine. "Elaine, I am so glad you stayed."

He took the fork and poked at the plate.

"Trent, can I ask you something?"

"Uh huh," he replied. "Of course."

"Do you remember what you said last night?"

"That I'm sorry, and I mean that, Elaine. I am sorry for the intrusion into Sabal Palms and for trying to be aggressive about the development plans."

"Do you remember anything else you said?"

"Of course. You were the first person I wanted to tell."

"Oh?"

"He saved me and gave me a second chance. When He was there, there was a glow all around Him in the dark. He said, 'Trent, you have My Spirit. I have called you. *Fear not, for I have redeemed you; I have called you by name, you are mine.*'[5] Those were His exact words. I knew in my heart that He knows how lost I have been. He came for me. He wants me to work for Him now, to put Him first."

"You are the one." Elaine's eyes teared up.

"What?"

"The verse I read yesterday morning. The Shepherd left to look for the one missing sheep, the one that went astray. That is you."

"I knew you would understand. I have so much to do."

"You have the rest of your life, Trent. You are young. You can do everything you want to do."

---

5   Isaiah 43:1

"I can't express . . . " Trent's lip was quivering. "I can't tell you how much I missed Him." He cried and reached for a tissue. "But now, I feel—I know—He is *in* me. I feel Him."

Elaine waited for Trent to collect himself. "It's like nothing I have ever experienced. I feel . . . clean. I feel . . . loved."

"I know that feeling, Trent. I know His presence."

"Elaine, will you help me? I want to make things right, starting with Sabal Palms."

Chapter Eighteen

Shirley spent the night in the only hotel room available that had a king suite. She was disappointed that there was no room service to speak of and only a small coffee pot in the room. She would go out for breakfast before she went to the hospital. *Dump of a hotel. Only has a breakfast buffet. Not eating that stuff.*

She made herself a cup of bland, watered-down coffee and promptly begin calling each of the investors. *It definitely is not Kona coffee.*

"Hello, Mr. Dinero, this is Shirley. Sorry I didn't call last night; it was late by the time I got into my room. I just wanted to check in with you and let you know that Trent is alive and in intensive care."

"I see; that's understandable. Did you speak with him?"

"No, not last night. I am going out today to see him."

"Will you call me after your visit?"

"Of course. I will call each of you today."

"Now, Shirley, let's not talk with him yet about our arrangement. No need to get him talking about business or upset about any business deals, for that matter. Let's wait until he is out of the hospital. Unless he brings it up, I would prefer we meet with him face-to-face and show him the revised proposal."

"Of course. It may be a while before he is discharged. Do you all want to fly out here when he is discharged?"

"Let's just play it by ear."

"Okay."

"Are you going to call each of us this morning?"

"Yes, sir. And I will touch base after I see him later today as well."

"Thank you, Shirley."

Shirley followed the call to Dinero with a call to Green and then Franklin. Each of the investors made the same request—meet together to present the revised proposal to Trent and not talk business right away. The exact repetition of each request meant only one thing— the three other investors had been talking without her. What was worse, they were likely talking *about* her. *Should I be worried? Will they want to back out of our agreement? Cancel the venture completely? Have I blown the deal for Trent?*

Shirley found a café nearby and went in for breakfast. She would drive out to the hospital as soon as she ate.

She was seated right away and given a menu. The list of options was nothing she expected to see on a breakfast menu. *What is barbacoa? What are chilaquiles? Ah, here we go, eggs and bacon—wait, in a tortilla?*

Frustrated, she called the waitress and asked for just eggs and toast, which was delivered within minutes.

"Would you like Cholula sauce?"

"I have no idea what that is, so, no, I think this is fine. Oh, and more coffee please."

"Sí."

Probably should have gone to the island to find a hotel—one with room service.

Shirley's drive to the hospital was short. She arrived at the lobby and asked about Trent.

"Excuse me, can you tell me if Trent Fortune has been moved to a regular room?"

"Let me check for you. No, he remains in intensive care. You may check in with the nurse's station on the fourth floor."

"Thank you."

Reluctantly, Shirley stopped at the nurse's station once again and asked if she could visit Trent.

"No. I'm sorry; his guest is still there. The doctor will be by in a few minutes and let us know if Mr. Fortune is ready to be moved. You may sit in the intensive care waiting room."

"Thank you."

***

Elaine helped Trent eat a few bites of breakfast.

"Thank you, Elaine. You should get you something to eat."

The door opened, and Dr. Salazar appeared.

"Well, good morning, Trent. It is good to see you are back with us. Let's have a look."

The doctor examined Trent's chart, then gave him a brief exam.

"You are improving. How would you like to be moved into a different room?"

"That will be fine," Trent said.

"I will put the request in as soon as one is available; they will get you down there. You are going to be moved to the second floor to a critical care room. You will be watched more closely there but can have more than one guest at a time if you like."

"Okay," Trent said. "Is it possible to get some breakfast in here for Elaine?"

"Yes. She can go to the cafeteria while we finish your exam." The doctor turned to Elaine and said, "He won't be moved for a while, so just come back up here when you are finished."

"Thank you."

Elaine left Trent's intensive care room and walked to the elevator. While waiting, a woman approached her.

"Hello, excuse me, were you just in Mr. Fortune's room?"

"Yes."

Shirley's first thought was to wonder what Trent wanted with this significantly older woman. Why was this Elaine Smith important to him? Why did he want to see only her?

"Allow me to introduce myself." Shirley extended her hand. "I'm his assistant, Shirley Matthews."

"Hello, nice to meet you. I am Elaine Smith."

The elevator chimed.

"Mind if I go down with you?"

"Okay."

Once in the elevator, Shirley began a string of questions that Elaine was too exhausted to answer in much detail.

"Tell me, how do you know Trent? I'm sorry. It's just that I haven't heard him mention your name."

Elaine laughed. "I'm not surprised that he hasn't mentioned me. I'm just an ordinary citizen from Sabal Palms."

"Oh? And then, well, where did you meet?"

Elaine began to feel uncomfortable and was glad when the elevator landed on the first floor.

"I met him the first time, along with many other citizens, at a town meeting, where he explained his project."

"The first time?"

"Yes. And then I saw him again at a friend's party."

"And what do you think of the development ideas for Sabal Palms?"

Elaine felt even more interrogated. "I'm sorry, Shirley, but I must get a little something to eat and then get back up to see Trent. Perhaps we can visit another time."

"Yes, I would like to talk more."

Elaine turned from the elevator and walked to the cafeteria.

***

Elaine returned to Trent's intensive care room without seeing Shirley again.

"Glad you're back," Trent said.

"Trent, I am happy to be here as long as you like, but I am wondering what exactly I am here for."

"Because I knew you were the one person who would understand."

"Understand what?"

"About coming to Christ."

"How did you know that about me?"

"I heard your story last year about Frankie the Gun. Every investor on the East Coast, everyone in Florida—we all heard it. We all talked about it."

"Really?"

"Yes. A few of my investors—two who are interested in Sabal Palms—worked with some of Frankie the Gun's New York associates."

"Small world, I suppose."

"Isn't it?"

"Trent, speaking of that, I met someone downstairs who wants to see you."

"Shirley, I'm guessing."

"Yes."

"I am not ready to see her yet. Before I see her, I wanted to settle a few things with you."

"Okay. Now I am very curious."

"Elaine, I know that you and many of your friends are against the development of Sabal Palms."

"Well, yes—"

"Let me explain. Elaine, the last few days, after my visit from Christ, I am a new person. I have truly been given a second chance, and He asked me to work for Him, to focus on Him now."

"Trent, you know you will get a lot of pushback when you tell people you had a visit from Jesus."

"I expect it."

"It could be a fight."

"I expect that, too. Nonetheless, I am going to do exactly what He asked. It is the reason I am still here."

"I understand that part. But how are you going to do this? To change and work only for Him?"

"There will be many different parts. So many projects I need to change. But first, I can change this one, the one for Sabal Palms, before any damage is done."

"How?"

"If you have time, I would like very much if you and I could go over my plans and let me change them. I want your input. I want someone who knows the people. And if you have knowledge of the environment or know someone who champions animals, let's ask them also."

"I do. I have a friend who is very active in that cause—Mary."

"And, Elaine, I want to change the idea of developing the beach in front of your house. But most importantly, I want to help the church on the shore to stay the church on the shore. In fact, I can provide funds to repair or remodel, whatever they need. But we can talk about all those details as we go. For right now, I want to ask, will you help me? Will you help me with this revision?"

"Of course, Trent. I would be delighted to do so."

"Thank you."

"Trent, what about Shirley? She is asking to see you."

"I will talk to her when I am moved into the other room. But I don't want to talk about business yet. Once you and I outline my revised plan, I will talk with Shirley and the investors. For right now, let's keep this idea just between you and me. As soon as I am discharged, would you be able to arrange a meeting with just a few people who can help us? Say, five or six? A small committee?"

"Okay. I know just the group."

"In the meantime, do you need to go home for a while? You have been here since yesterday."

"Well, I need to attend to my dog. Bonnie took care of her for me, but I need to go home for a bit and take care of her."

"Can you come back later this afternoon? I will be moved to the other room, take a nap, and be ready."

"How about three o'clock?"

"Perfect."

"What do I say to any questions? It is a little strange that you sent for me, given your history in Sabal Palms."

"We can stretch the truth a little. How about that I asked to see you because of our last meeting in the conference room? That I just wanted to ask more questions about the town?"

"I can try that one."

Elaine opened the door to leave, and Trent called her back.

"Oh, Elaine?"

"Yes?"

"Do you have a Bible you can bring me?"

"Yes. I do."

"Thank you."

***

Shirley waited. And waited. She checked with the nurse's station several times. She went to the cafeteria and ate lunch. She answered texts from the investors. The same messages went out to each one: "Waiting for Trent to be moved so he can have visitors." She read every paper she found in the waiting room and thumbed through several magazines.

At last, a nurse came to the waiting area, "Mr. Fortune is being moved now. You may see him in room 208 in about thirty minutes. If you like, you might want to move down to the second floor waiting room."

"Thank you."

Shirley checked her watch every five minutes. Exactly thirty minutes after the nurse announced the room change, Shirley knocked on room 208.

"Come in."

"Trent. Oh, my goodness. Look at you. All of these tubes and wires."

He laughed. "They took half of them out already."

"Are you okay? Do you need anything?"

"No, I'm fine, thanks. I appreciate you coming to Texas to check up on me."

"What happened? I mean, the plane and everything."

"What I remember, there was lightning. And then there was water, and I was in it. All the stuff that actually happened during the crash, I don't remember."

"I heard there was an explosion."

"Really? Guess I was out for that part."

"You are really lucky. You got a second chance."

He smiled. "Yes, indeed I did. And, Shirley, I know the office has been in good hands while I have been away. Thank you."

"Is there anything else you need to tell me? I don't want to bring up business—"

"Good. I don't either. Not sure my head could take it right now."

"I'm sorry. We can wait. Just know that everyone is asking about you."

"Everyone?"

"The investors, your other business associates, you know."

"Yes. Okay. Thank you and tell them thank you for asking about me."

"I will."

"Are you going to stay in town?"

"As long as you need me."

"Maybe in a few days, we can talk. Right now, I am just not up to it. In the meantime, you can take a little break. Go to the island."

"I just might do that. I would like to switch hotels. Maybe I will find a new hotel on the island."

"There are some nice ones over there. You can catch some rays, swim—"

"I get the picture. I will tour around to some of the places you spoke about in your last visits. You have my cell number. Call if you need anything or want me to pick you up when they discharge you."

"Okay. Thanks. Enjoy yourself."

Chapter Nineteen

Elaine no more than put her foot on her deck when Bonnie ran behind her and bombarded her with an arsenal of questions.

"What did he want? What happened? Has he lost his mind? Why did he ask for you? Spill it, Elaine; spill it. Don't leave out a single detail."

"Hello to you, too, Bonnie."

"It is just so strange. You are the one leading the fight against him and his development. Why you?"

"Bonnie, he is still in recovery. I'm not sure he is thinking at one-hundred percent. But he did want to talk a little about the development in Sabal Palms."

"Really? Trying to make friends with the enemy now, is he?"

Elaine unlocked her front door. "Hey, Bella. Hi, girl." Bella wagged her tail and went crazy jumping all around. "I missed you, too." She picked up Bella, who squirmed nonstop with excitement. "Hey, Bonnie, I need to walk Bella. Want to walk?"

"Sure."

"Thanks for taking care of her yesterday."

"No problem. She was a good girl."

It was good to be out in the fresh air with the scent of salt and water in the air. Try as she might, Elaine could not keep Bonnie from talking about Trent and the development.

"We have the petition ready to go," Bonnie said. "We printed several hundred copies."

"Bonnie, let's hold off on that for a while. At least let Trent get back on his feet. He has just been moved from intensive care to critical care. He has about fifty different tubes and wires hooked up."

"Elaine, I had no idea. I mean, I wasn't thinking about how badly he must have been injured. Of course. We can wait. If he is in the hospital, I guess the development is on hold, anyway."

"Yes. He had quite a traumatic experience. Can you imagine? Crashing and then being out to sea for days."

"Heaven's sakes, no. I can't comprehend that at all. It's horrible."

"I think he is having a hard time, you know, getting back to reality."

"What? What do you mean?"

"He seemed a little foggy. He said he didn't remember much at all about the crash and that he didn't want to speak with his investors for a few more days. I think we are safe to wait on taking any action with the commissioners. We have time."

"Of course."

"Bonnie, can you do something for me?"

"What can I do?"

"When we finish our walk, I would love a nap, and then I am going back over to the hospital to check on Trent. He asked if I would. You mind calling the rest of our group and filling them in on where things stand? Ask them to hold off. We can meet again in a day or so and see how Trent feels and what he wants to do."

"I will call them, and we can set a time to meet, say, day after tomorrow? Will that work?"

"That would be wonderful."

***

At three p.m., Elaine knocked on Trent's hospital door.

"Come in."

"Hello. You look a little more rested. And a couple fewer tubes?"

"Yes, they took out a few more."

Unloading her large bag, she said, "I'm loaded with paper, pencils, calculator, and, most important, a Bible."

"What? No laptop?" He laughed.

"No, sorry. Maybe tomorrow."

"It's okay. I'm more of a pencil-and-paper guy myself."

"Nice room. Nice flowers. And lots of them. Wow!"

"You know, the funny thing is, I don't know these people. Pick a card, any card, and read it to me."

"Let's see—nice roses from Mr. and Mrs. Billingsly."

"Not a clue."

"How about these lilies? Mr. Wentworth?"

"Nope." Trent grinned sheepishly. "You get the picture."

"I do. Anyone who hears of a surviving plane crash victim in the hospital sends flowers?"

"Not really. See, the sad thing is, Elaine, they know who I am, but I'm not sure I've ever met them. And if I did, I was too busy or thought myself too important to pay attention to them. That is a sad, sad shell of a man." He looked down. "But that is going to change. From now on, I want to get to know people. Work with them."

"I think you will enjoy it. But Trent, why didn't you want to get to know people before?"

"Never cared. Never cared about anything but money."

"Hmm, any idea why?"

"I think I do. But maybe we should get started and talk about that on another day."

Sensing that Trent was uncomfortable, she moved ahead.

"Where do we start?" she asked.

"First, let's start with the church. I want to take it completely off the table, out of the proposal. And instead, I want to write a letter to the church offering a donation for whatever they might need."

"Right now, they need a pastor."

"Is there a way to fund that?" Trent asked.

"Like maybe an increase in the salary offered perhaps?"

Trent thought for a moment. "Yes. Wait, I know. I will offer a CD with interest, and the interest can be added to the salary incentive. It will be a large enough amount and in a structured, risk-free account to guard against loss, so it continues to add to the salary fund year after year."

"That would be an amazing offer, I'm sure."

Trent smiled. "We are off to a good start."

"Next?"

He moved on. "Let's talk about the golf course."

"Okay. I am curious about that. It involves so many of the homeowners' properties. How would that be revised?"

"Here is where I will need your friend's help. Mary?"

"Yes."

"If the people of Sabal Palms want to have the golf course, it must respect all of the wildlife refuge boundaries, and perhaps we can donate a bit more land. We will see what Mary thinks. And I want to change the design of the course so that it infringes on no one's property."

"Adriana will like this part very much."

"Now, as for the inn, restaurant, and so on, I think I can get an environmental consultant to examine each of those structures."

They worked through the evening. Trent asked Elaine to return the following day to continue.

"What time should I get here?"

"How about nine? Maybe I will get out of here tomorrow." Pulling on one of the remaining tubes, Trent said, "They took out most of these things. I hope to be free of all of these by morning."

"See you at nine."

"Before you go, can you put your phone number on this paper? Just in case I need to contact you?"

"Of course."

"And do you mind handing me that Bible?"

Elaine placed the Bible in Trent's hand. "Everything you need is in here."

"I know that now."

***

Elaine sat down at her typewriter, happy to be home early enough to have writing time. She jotted down a few notes. So much had happened in the past few days. First, the whole town had rallied around to fight off the impending intrusion of high-dollar investors who threatened to change her world and her church. Funds had been collected and were waiting to be used to hire attorneys to win the battle. Then from nowhere, tragedy struck a lone pilot out over the Gulf of Mexico. A miraculous recovery happened just a few days before, which included a reported visit from Jesus over the water. Trent, now starting his second chance at life, was working with her to change the development plans. No one knew the whole story. No one could know yet. All in time. Telling the story was up to Trent. But she couldn't help but reflect on these miracles. She knew Trent had experienced a Divine intervention. He would be forever changed.

Elaine wrote a devotional about trust and how hard it is to always know that God will work things out. She thought back on all her efforts—meetings to organize, raising funds, and writing a petition. And in the end, God already had a plan. She forgot that He works behind the scenes.

Then, she had an amazing recollection of Trent's words. He had been saved. He had been born again right out there in the Gulf of Mexico. She had written many things that impacted the hearts of people, motivated them to apologize, repent, go back to church, and make amends. But hearing a new believer, a person who was just born again, describe his own experience was like nothing she had felt before. Once again, she committed to bring others to Christ. It was her purpose. It was the call of all Christians.

She sat in silence. She prayed for guidance. She thanked God for His gifts of witnessing, and she thanked Him for her gift of writing. She prayed that He would lead her in the direction of making a difference.

Elaine rolled the clean, white paper up to the proper position. Then, something unexplainable happened. Her fingers began flying over the keys, typing out one word after another. She did not understand the meaning, but she knew these words were meant for Trent. She continued at a rapid pace. And then, there were no more words. She knew it was complete, yet she did not understand exactly what the content meant.

At 2:30, she turned off her desk lamp and called it a day.

***

The next morning, Elaine took Bella out for her morning walk. Bonnie was already waiting outside.

"Good morning, Bonnie."

"Hi, Elaine. Ready? I need to get more exercise! I skipped my walk the other day, and my blood sugar told on me!" Bonnie laughed.

"Let's go. Bella is ready."

No matter how many mornings Elaine walked on the beach, she never tired of it. Always peaceful, even on slightly windy days or days of approaching storms. The waves across her feet, the laughing gulls, the salty air, and the diving pelicans always kept her centered.

"Bella, leave that crab alone," Elaine admonished. Bella scampered up from the waves.

"So, what are you doing today?" Bonnie asked.

"Not sure. Trent asked me to come over. I hope he's in better shape and will be released soon."

"After that, we can decide when to get the group together. Oh, I wanted to tell you yesterday, Mary and Adriana put the money we have collected into a savings account. They wanted all our names on it, but the rest of us didn't see any reason for that. Mary or Adriana can access it when we need it."

"I think that was a great idea."

"Good."

"Want to walk down to the church?"

"If you have time before you drive into Brownsville."

"Sure."

Elaine examined the church differently today. She wanted to check for any structural repairs needed. She and Bonnie walked inside briefly for a quick glance so Elaine might report back to Trent. She noticed the aging paint inside and out, the old carpet, and the cracked tile floors. She overlooked all these minor cosmetic needs in the past. She made mental notes, and then they headed back to their cottages.

Elaine showered and dressed. Walking toward the door, she stopped when her phone buzzed.

"Hello?"

"Hi, Elaine, Trent."

"Good morning. Just on my way out."

"Can you do a huge favor for me?"

"What can I help you with?"

"My notebook for the development project is at the hotel. I contacted the desk, and they were to send the bellman to retrieve it for me. If you don't mind, can you go over to the island and pick it up? It will help us today."

"No problem at all. I will go over before I come to the hospital. Might be a little later getting to Brownsville."

"No worries. The front desk is expecting you. The binder has your name on it. Oh, and I asked for another change of clothes. They should have those waiting as well."

"I will be happy to get those for you. I will see you in a bit."

Elaine picked up her car keys and then remembered the pages she had written the night before. She put the pages in a file and took them with her. If she felt the timing was correct and an opportunity presented itself, she would give the pages to Trent.

***

Trent was alert, unhooked from every wire and tube, and waiting for Elaine when she arrived.

Elaine slowly poked her head inside the door. "Good morning."

"Come on in. Good morning."

"You look well. Except for the bruises and stitches on your forehead, you look good as new."

"Minor details. I am alive. I am so blessed."

"Yes, we are blessed to have another day. Here is your binder."

"Thank you. It will help us in our progress today, Elaine."

Elaine sat down and disappeared behind two tall flower arrangements placed on the bedside table. She opened the binder. "Where should we start?"

"Maybe by moving some of these flowers around, we can see each other while we work," he said with a laugh.

"It looks like you had more deliveries."

"I think it was a delivery truck full!"

Elaine laughed.

"Say, Elaine, can these flowers be donated somehow?"

"I don't know. Any ideas?"

"Are there people here in the hospital who might not have any flowers? Or maybe they just have one flower arrangement and another one would brighten their day?"

"I am sure there are people who would appreciate these flowers. Want me to ask?"

"No, no. I'll ring the nurse and ask."

The nurse appeared promptly. She assured Trent the flowers could be taken to other rooms and would be appreciated by people who had few or no family or visitors.

"Good idea, Trent. You are starting off your new life by a great action, sharing the cheer."

Trent smiled.

"Now that we've taken care of the flower situation, what's next?" Elaine asked.

"I want to go over the binder with you. Not so much the financial part, but the actual plan and the drawings for the golf course."

"Okay."

"Look at section two. That's where we can start."

Together, Trent and Elaine turned through each section. He told her where to write notes on the pages, and they both wrote down notes on their yellow pads.

"Hi, Trent," Dr. Salazar said as he entered the room.

"Hello," Trent replied. "This is my good friend, Elaine Smith. We are just doing a little work."

"Sorry to interrupt. But I have good news. If you continue to make good progress, you will be discharged tomorrow. If you have any reason to need to stay, we will put you in a regular room. But right now, the regular rooms are full, so you can stay right here."

"That's great."

"Don't get carried away. When you get discharged, remember you have had a *major* trauma. Don't go kite-boarding or hang gliding or anything."

Trent laughed. "Promise."

"Good deal. I will come by once more tonight, and then I'll check with the nurses in the morning about your discharge."

"Thanks, Doc."

Elaine and Trent worked steadily until lunchtime. At Trent's request, a hospital volunteer went to the cafeteria on the first floor and picked up two daily specials of grilled chicken salads.

"I never thought hospital food would taste this good. Well, it is better than the soup and pudding and eggs they gave me," he joked.

"It is pretty good. I didn't realize I was hungry. Say, this must be the first real food you have had since . . . "

"The day I crashed. Yes. That evening, I had a wonderful meal on the island. I would have eaten more if I had known," he remarked.

Following lunch, they got right back to work. After a few hours, Elaine said, "Trent, you look a little tired."

"To tell you the truth, I am kind of tired of all of these project plans and notes. Maybe we should call it a day? We have just about finished, anyway."

"Oh, sure. I need to get back and tend to Bella. I'm sure she wants to go for her evening walk."

"You sure love that little dog."

Reaching for her keys, she said, "She's a sweetheart."

When Elaine stood, the file with the pages she had written for Trent fell to the floor. "Oh, sorry," she said.

"Is that something I stuck in the binder we need to look over?"

"Actually, it's something I wrote last night. I'm not sure, but I think I am to give it to you."

"Really? For me?"

"Yes. I don't know exactly how this relates to you, but I think it is for you." Elaine handed him the paper.

"Okay. Thanks. I will look it over this evening."

"I will get out of your hair. See you tomorrow?"

"Yes. Hopefully, it will be for a ride back to the island."

Chapter Twenty

Elaine picked Trent up at the hospital the following morning and drove him to his hotel. She escorted him up to his penthouse suite. She was taken by the view across the Gulf of Mexico.

"This is a breathtaking view."

"It is. Looking out there, it's hard to believe a couple of days ago, I was flying over the island, the water, the bay . . . And then, I wasn't."

"And here you are, a new person."

"A second chance." He smiled. "Elaine, I know that I have been given a second chance. I read the pages you gave me yesterday. The words are exactly what I need to do. But how did you know? I have never talked about this with anyone."

"I'm not sure. The words—well, they just came to me. But you don't have to explain anything to me. I am thankful they meant something to you. I know it's hard to believe that words could just be put in my head like that. I'm sure it seems unbelievable."

"Unbelievable? Elaine, you are talking to someone who was rescued by Jesus Himself over the sea. You are talking to someone who survived a plane crash, explosion, dehydration, near-starvation, lightning, and who knows what else! Of course, I believe that you were inspired by God to write something meant for me."

Elaine laughed. "You make a good point."

"I want to tell you what it means. You will understand it all. I want you to know why."

"Why what?"

"Why I will need to return to Georgia in a few days to my parents' homeplace."

"Okay."

"I haven't told anyone else in my company, or really anyone. When I left Georgia eighteen years ago, I didn't leave on good terms. My father was abusive to me. Physically and mentally. He loved his church, but he loved alcohol more. He was an awful man. When he went to church, it was always to ask for forgiveness and to start all over again."

"I'm so sorry."

"And the worst part, I blamed my mother. I believed she could have stopped him. Or she and I could have run away. But now I understand that she did the best she could do. She didn't have a choice. He was hurting her, too. And now, I know from your writing, this second chance I have been given is for relationships, also. The words mean I am to go back to my parents and forgive them, ask for their forgiveness, and start a relationship again. I don't even know if it is possible, but I have to try."

"That's what the second-chance sentences meant. A chance to renew and revive love. Thank you for telling me, Trent. I know you will make your second chance at life count for your parents—and others. You will make a difference in peoples' lives—starting right here in Sabal Palms."

Trent smiled. "I hope so."

Elaine prayed Trent's new life would continue. She wondered if, over time, he might fall back into his previous ways of wanting to make money, of being consumed with increasing his wealth. The ability to travel wherever, do whatever—would he miss it? Would he want to have the financial freedom to buy airplanes, for example?

"Trent, there is something I have been curious about. Will you fly a plane again?"

"Yes. I enjoy flying."

"Will you buy another plane?"

"Eventually. I'm sure insurance will cover the one that crashed. But I have others and two pilots on retainer in Miami. When I am ready to go somewhere, I can call them. But right now, I want to stay here and work on this second chance with Sabal Palms. I think it is time."

"Time?"

"I think I'm ready to meet with your group, the people from town who are interested in this project."

"Keep in mind, my friends in Sabal Palms were interested in the development project because they wanted to fight it."

He nodded. "I understand completely. We can go over the changes and ask for their input. I prefer to get the details nailed down with your group to get their approval and further suggestions before I meet with the investors."

"Are you up to driving over to Sabal Palms?"

"I was thinking we could meet here. The suite has a conference room, and I can have some refreshments brought in."

"That would be very nice. When do you want to do this?"

"How about this afternoon? Would that be too soon?"

"Let me make a few calls. What time?"

"Two o'clock work for you?"

"See you then."

***

Elaine was halfway across the causeway when her phone rang. She answered on her hands-free car monitor. "Hello."

"Hi, Elaine."

"Oh, Bonnie, I was about to call you."

"We're all over at Mary's house. Want to come over—if you are finished at the hospital?"

"Sure. I should be there in about fifteen minutes."

Arriving at Mary's house fifteen minutes later, Elaine rang the doorbell.

"Come on in, stranger," Mary yelled.

"Hi. How is everyone?"

Ramon stood up and hugged Elaine. "We haven't seen you in nearly three days!"

"Good to be with you all."

Bonnie blurted, "Well, I have seen you on the beach; but tell us, now that Trent is out, what are we going to do? Are we ready to start the petitions? Can we go door to door?"

Mary chimed in, "I'm ready. Have on my walking shoes and I am ready for battle!"

Billy concurred, "I can take the downtown section."

"Wait, slow down just a minute," Elaine protested.

In a loud voice with additional hand gestures, Adriana exclaimed, "Elaine, we can't waste any time. This is my property that is on the line. Like Antony used to say—God rest his soul"—she crossed her chest—"we need to prevent things that are in our control. And right now, we are armed and ready, so let's move forward!"

"Okay. Stop."

Bonnie said, "For Pete's sakes, let Elaine speak!"

"Trent Fortune would like for us all to come in for a meeting—"

"Like the last time when he wouldn't give us the time of day?" Adriana asked.

"For crying out loud, let her finish," Mary said.

"He would like us to go to his hotel at two this afternoon. We can ride together in two cars."

"Meet? In his hotel?" Billy asked.

"Yes," Elaine said. "He wants to discuss something with our group."

Everyone was silent for a moment.

"Okay," Adriana said. "I'm curious enough to go. I'm in. Let's have some lunch and then head over there."

Thankfully, Mary was able to put together a buffet of deli meats and cheeses. She and Bonnie threw a salad together. Adriana fixed the tea, and the group ate quickly.

***

Adriana, Mary, and Bonnie piled into Elaine's car. Billy joined Ramon and Maria in their oversized truck. Even though the traffic across the causeway moved at a slow pace, they arrived at the hotel on time.

Inside the lobby, they walked toward the elevator. "Not that one," Elaine corrected. "The penthouse elevator."

"Penthouse? Well, excuse me," Mary said.

"Mary, behave yourself," Bonnie chided.

The group made it to the penthouse and stood before Trent's hotel room door.

Elaine knocked.

"Please come in."

Seeing Trent's bruises and stitches, Mary gasped. "You look like you had a time. Are you sure you feel like having company?"

"Yes, please, there is a conference table down this hallway."

Mary and Bonnie "oohed and "ahhed" with every step into the suite. They took their seats around the table. Trent, pulling a chair out beside him, said, "Elaine, do you mind sitting over here by me?"

Elaine took the chair. Trent handed her the tablets and the binder. Next, he passed around hotel letterhead paper to the group.

"Mr. Fortune, do you mind telling us what this is about?" Billy asked.

"Billy Wrangle, big fan. Nice to see you again. Please, call me Trent."

"Thanks."

"I know that in the past couple of weeks, we haven't been on the same side of planning for Sabal Palms."

The room was still. No one said anything. No one moved. All waited to hear what Trent would say next.

"Let me start by telling each of you, my initial ideas about Sabal Palms have changed. I know you heard about the plane crash. I will share with you now exactly what happened. I would ask complete discretion until I have had a chance to meet with my investors, but I wanted to speak with you first. I have not spoken to the press about the crash, although I have had requests. I would ask that you each keep what we are talking about today to yourselves. I want to be sure of the final plan for Sabal Palms before anything is announced. And no one needs to hear any details about the crash. There will be investigations and questions by the insurance company, I'm sure. The less said about the crash or what we are planning for Sabal Palms, the better."

Bonnie looked at Mary, who looked at Adriana, all seemingly questioning what was happening. Billy shrugged his shoulders, and Ramon and Maria looked questioningly at each other. It was clear, *nothing* of what Trent said was clear.

"I don't really remember the crash of the plane into the water. I remember lightning. I don't remember hearing the explosion, although I have heard there was one. What I do remember—and I know this in my heart—I was given a second chance at life. The doctors told me it was a miracle that I survived. I know they are right about that. It was a miracle, and I believe it was God's will for me to be here with you to apologize and to meet with you now to plan together to help Sabal Palms. I want to be sure I understand one thing before we go any further. Are the people of Sabal Palms interested in having a company put in a golf course to generate revenue? Are you interested in having a beach development of some sort?"

Mary couldn't hold back another second. "But what about the church? The New Age religion?"

"Oh, you know about that. You all did your homework. It is true that I was once influenced by that group. I know now that those were false prophets. Elaine was kind enough to bring a Bible to me at the hospital, and if I wasn't spending my time the last few days planning for the community with Elaine, I was reading the Bible night and day. I understand now, more than ever, there is only one God. And I would like to include the church in the funding for improvement, but only what the current church needs. Elaine and I discussed the need to increase the salary for the position of pastor. I believe this will help to recruit a good, Christian pastor."

Mary asked, "And what about the golf course? Will that change?"

And Bonnie added, "And the beach?"

Trent laughed. "Elaine, you were correct, this *is* the group we need to help us. Mary, correct?" he asked gesturing to Mary.

"Yes?"

"I was told you can help with the campaign to improve the habitats and preserve the wildlife?"

"Yes. I volunteer and know the various committees who oversee the wildlife, birding, and marine life campaigns."

"Excellent. We will need your input."

Ramon spoke up next. "Now, hold on just a minute. Let's say we are interested in raising money for the town of Sabal Palms. The town needs the money, that's certain. We are still recovering from Jada. And the townspeople would like to have the infrastructure improved and made more hurricane-resistant. That said, exactly what are you planning to do?"

"I am asking for your help in revising my plans. Elaine has offered her input. I would like to go over what she and I have discussed. If we are in agreement to move forward with development and a revised plan is agreed upon investing the money where you, the citizens of Sabal Palms want, I will go forward with a presentation to the other investors to implement these changes."

Ramon continued, "So, you are on our side?"

Trent laughed again. "Yes, I want to work with you."

Adriana, who had been reserved to this point, said, "But, Trent, I know in the past, my husband Antony—God rest his soul"—she crossed her chest—"had business deals that seemed to change, but then he was later double-crossed. They changed their minds and became greedy for their own wishes."

"That is unfortunate, Adriana; but I can tell you, with all sincerity, I am only going forward with what you and the other community members want to do. I don't need money. I want to use the funds I have accumulated to improve the world, starting with Sabal Palms. My desire is no longer for money, but to make things better for others. Look, I was given a second chance, a chance to start over. This time, I want to do it right."

Billy spoke next. "I want to apologize if I sound doubtful. I have known many people in Nashville, involved in the music scene, and they have had people turn on them when they least expected it. Not that I believe you would, Trent, but what about the other people in your investment group? Will they go along with any changes we want to make?"

Before Trent could respond, Bonnie asked, "And aren't some of those investors also interested in changing the church from Christian to New Age?"

"I understand your concerns. And we should all be concerned. I know the other investors will be a problem. My goal is for us to put together a plan that they can approve. I don't mind a compromise or two on something like total yardage of the golf course or square footage of the restaurant. But I will not compromise on the church. That is a deal breaker."

"Then following along with this train of thought—and not meaning to be too nosy about the money—in the end, will your share of the investment be enough leverage to move in this direction?" Billy asked.

On this point, Trent was quiet. He scanned their faces. He finally said, "In the current structure of this investment, I do not think it will be enough. It will take some financial wizardry, but the deal can be put together in such a way that I would increase my share, providing the partners would agree."

Elaine felt a twinge of anxiety. Would this deal work? Would Sabal Palms be able to fight off the other investors?

Sensing the sudden change of mood in the room, Trent replied, "We have to join forces here. I know that God is on our side. I believe we should trust Him. It will work out in the end. Financially and every other way possible, I will do what it takes to make this work. Now, shall we get started?"

For the remainder of the day, the group worked tirelessly. Every detail was scrutinized. Every property on the golf course plan was examined. The properties that were not required were scratched from the "Ask to Buy" list. The beachfront property was relocated further north, where there were no houses. It would add fifteen minutes to the shuttle ride from the inn at the golf course, but it would allow those homeowners, or cottage owners, to remain in a secluded section that would be far away from the beachside café.

The group reviewed the proposal for long-term funding of a pastor's salary. In addition, Trent proposed improvements and upgrades in both the little church and the pastor's living quarters.

The group was served an early, light dinner to munch as they worked. By the time all the changes were noted, the group witnessed the sunset from the penthouse windows.

"I know we are all exhausted, especially Trent," Elaine said. "And we need to get back across the causeway to Sabal Palms. The only thing we need to do now is ask you, Trent, what is the next step?"

"I will arrange for the investors to fly in tomorrow morning. Let's have a meeting in the Sabal Palms town office meeting room tomorrow afternoon. We will put everything on the table, the plans between our committee here and the investors. If it goes well, we can inform the rest of the town. If not, we will work on phase two of our plan."

"And what is phase two?" Ramon asked.

"How to go into battle with the investors."

Chapter Twenty-One

Elaine had to admit her emotions had been on shaky ground the last few weeks. It started with Bonnie's news about her lab tests, followed by all the business with the development plan, the surprise visit by Mary's long-lost cousin, the plane crash, and the last few days spent helping Trent. Just when she thought she was feeling better, anxiety crept in again. This time, it was because of the last-minute meeting called with Trent's investors.

She prayed she would accept God's will, no matter what the end result would be for Sabal Palms. She knew the ultimate outcome would fit into God's bigger picture somehow. It was beyond her understanding at this point in time.

Elaine's phone buzzed.

"Hello, Bonnie."

"Well, I am totally bumfuzzled. You aren't going to believe what is happening outside my door."

"My goodness, what?"

"Those blasted surveyors are here."

"What?"

"Yes. They are traipsing up and down in front of my cottage. And a drone just flew by."

"Bonnie, do you want me to call Trent to see what is happening?"

"No, no, I don't want to bother him. He's probably on his way over to our meeting by now. We'll see him within the hour, and I can ask him then. Have you looked outside your door in the last few minutes?"

"Haven't had a chance. I was just getting out of the shower. But I will check before I pick you up."

"See you in a few minutes."

Elaine slapped on some tropical scent lotion and picked out a pair of blue capris and a Hawaiian-print shirt. She picked out a pair of aqua earrings and her silver-and-aquamarine bracelet. She was ready.

Elaine locked her cottage door and was buzzed by a large drone.

"Bonnie was right. We are being invaded," she muttered.

She arrived at Bonnie's house and found Bonnie on her deck taking pictures of the surveyors and the drones. Elaine honked her horn, and Bonnie ran down her steps and out to the car.

"Whew, I forgot how hard it is to run down steps in flip-flops." Bonnie sat in the front seat and huffed.

"I see what you mean, Bonnie. They're everywhere. The surveyors were out front, and a drone was hovering just off the beach in front of my cottage."

"We will get to the bottom of this. It is either that Trent's previous plans were not canceled or worse," Bonnie said.

"Worse?"

With worry in her tone, Bonnie said, "Those other investors might just be marching ahead, as if Trent had no say-so."

"Guess we'll know soon enough," Elaine replied.

***

Trent was the first to arrive at the town hall meeting room. Elaine, Bonnie, and Mary followed. Adriana, Billy, Ramon, and Maria completed the team.

"Good afternoon, everyone," Trent said. "Looks like the investors are running a little late. My assistant, Shirley, sent a limo to pick them up in Harlingen. And Shirley will be arriving any minute."

The door opened and in stepped Shirley Matthews. Her expression of surprise told Elaine that the group from Sabal Palms was not who she expected to see.

"Hi, Trent. And is it Elaine? Is that right? We met at the hospital."

"Yes, hi, Shirley. Good to see you again."

"Trent, who are these fine people?"

Trent introduced each one and told Shirley a little bit about them. After a few pleasantries, Shirley turned her back on the group and faced Trent. She whispered, "What are they doing here? I thought it was us and the other investors?"

Before he could respond, the door opened again, and in walked Dinero, Green, and Franklin.

"Trent," Green said, "we have been worried. So glad to see you are out and about."

"Yes, you look good," Franklin agreed. "Well, you still look a little banged-up. Are you okay?"

"Yes, thank you. I am terrific."

"Good to hear. Trent, this town, Sabal Palms, is exactly as you described it," Dinero said. He then turned to the group and said, "Good afternoon."

Shirley asked again, "Trent, what is happening here?"

"I will explain." He turned to the investors and said, "Would you all please take a seat?"

Once everyone in the room was seated, he began. "As you all know, I have been here for almost two weeks now. I've been studying the community, talking with these fine people, walking, and—at least for a while—flying over the properties and all of the options for investment."

Uneasy laughter followed the statement of flying over the properties. The group quieted again.

"As you are aware, I had presented one proposal to you all before I left Miami. Since that time, I have revised the proposal to be more, shall we say, friendly for the townspeople."

Shirley looked puzzled. "How do you mean, Trent?"

"I have adjusted the golf-course proposal property boundaries so that the residents will not be asked to sell their land if they do not wish to do so. Second, I have relocated the beachfront investment property, and more importantly, I changed the proposal for the church."

Dinero asked, "What does all of that mean exactly? We liked the proposal as you presented it earlier."

"Yes, I'm sure you did. You all said as much. But you see, I hadn't asked the people here what they wanted to see in their community. Their preferences must be considered."

Shirley leaned toward Trent and whispered, "What has gotten into you? Are you out of your mind?"

Trent pulled away and said, "I know this may shock you, but if we want to have an ongoing relationship in this town, we should respect their wishes."

Franklin cleared his throat then spoke. "Trent, maybe this is some type of reaction to your . . . your trauma. But we had an understanding. We all agreed on the previous proposal. And in fact, if you want to change it in any way at all, Shirley had some other suggestions."

Blindsided, Trent turned to Shirley. "Oh? What were those suggestions?"

"I'm not sure we want to do this in a . . . public meeting."

"Shirley, these are the people we are working with. They have a right to hear every word of your suggestions. Is there something improper? Something underhanded you are proposing?"

"No, no, Trent. It's not that. It's, well, I found some additional ways to increase revenue. After all, we are *all* interested in making money, correct?"

"Not at the expense of taking away what these citizens have worked for all of their lives. Their homes, their privacy, their church. No. I am not interested in that."

Green jumped into the conversation. "Trent, you have to see the figures before you decide. Our wealth could be greatly increased. Shirley has taken funds and moved them around—"

"Without my knowledge? Before asking me, Shirley?"

"You were missing, and it makes more sense this way—"

"You just gave up on me returning? Your suggestions and my earlier suggestions do not make any sense for the people who live here. They are content living in Sabal Palms exactly like it is."

Franklin insisted, "Trent, Shirley's suggestions were outstanding. Your initial project is good, but what Shirley suggested will put the investment over the top. You should take a look at what she proposed to do. We were all so impressed that we agreed to make Shirley a partner—with your approval, of course."

Trent was silent. Elaine imagined he was weighing his options. The investors became uneasy. Elaine felt there was a stare-down happening, with the investors casting angry looks at the group from Sabal Palms.

After several minutes, Trent said, "I think I understand. I thank you all for coming all the way to Texas for this meeting. I will draft a new proposal, one that *I* will invest in. I will give each of you— even you, Shirley—a chance to invest in this new proposal. I will notify you when we can talk again. In the meantime, my previous proposal, the one we agreed on in Miami, is withdrawn. It is no longer on the table and will not be considered. Any funds you have already transferred will be returned. Any expenses will be reimbursed. If you don't want to accept the revised proposal once I submit it to you, you may counter with another proposal. Keep in mind, my company already owns a majority of the property needed for this venture. If you propose a project that I do not approve of, I will be willing to sell you my properties at a greatly increased price if the townspeople approve of the sell." Then turning to Shirley, he added, "Shirley, are you certain you want to go this direction with your proposal?"

She nodded.

"Very well. I will accept your resignation effective today."

The investors and Shirley quietly stood and left the room.

Elaine looked at Trent and asked, "Trent, what just happened?"

"It's a game, Elaine. Unfortunately, it is one we may not win."

Bonnie asked, "Trent, are your surveyors still at work? And drones?"

"You know what? I need to call my department of future investments and let them know to wait until our new plans are finalized. Then, we will wait and see what happens."

Billy asked, "What does that mean? We will see what happens?"

"Look, it is true that I own the properties. But the construction of the new facilities, the golf course, and so on, well, that was what the investors were funding. It will require a respectable amount of ready cash. I will have to figure out what to do without their money."

Billy continued, "What are the options? Any general ideas?"

"Generally speaking, very general, there are a few options. I can hold on to the land I have purchased and look for different investors, people who believe like we do; or I could possibly sell it, and nothing happens to Sabal Palms. Or . . . if I sell it, someone else comes in and buys the property—silent investors—and they develop it."

"Someone else would put in a golf course?" Ramon asked. "I kind of liked the idea of us having a golf course. It would be a good way to help our community."

"New investors, new property owners, could develop it however they wanted once the permits were approved. It could be condominiums, housing, any kind of commercial industry, whatever."

Elaine was less optimistic than she had been the day before. Looking at the group, she believed they all felt disheartened as well.

"Look," Trent said, "I am not giving up. I will study all possible options. We might be able to follow the revised plan we worked on yesterday. It's just a matter of money. We can look for other investors. Don't give up on this." He looked at Elaine. "Elaine knows this is very important to me. I think my narrow escape from death was a wakeup call. Elaine also knows that God was with me out there in the ocean.

230 Sabal Palms After the Storm

I was given a second chance, and I plan to use my resources to make this a better place. To make the world a better place. It might mean moving some funds or investments around, but I'm not giving up, and I don't want you to give up either."

Elaine felt a faint smile creep across her face and noticed the others did not look as distraught. She said, "Trent, I believe we can still do this. You tell us what you need. We can get the people behind this. The townspeople want to keep Sabal Palms, and the church, like it is. They only want to improve things, not change things to represent something we are not. They are not interested in becoming a big, high-traffic, tourist area. If there is a golf course or beach development, they want to help the environment and the endangered species. I know you want this also."

Mary said, "Trent, listen. I know we aren't a bunch of young whippersnappers, but we are dependable. We are enthusiastic about our community. We are all of the same faith. And we are dedicated hard-workers."

Bonnie added, "Whatever you need, Trent, we will help."

"Oh, for heaven's sakes," Adriana said, waving her hands. "Of course, we will help you, Trent."

Billy, Ramon, and Maria agreed with nodded heads. "Just tell us; we are here for you."

"Good. Let me talk with my people, my accountant—have him run the numbers and see exactly what we need. I will have my other office assistants send over a few documents. Can we meet day after tomorrow? That will give me time to get it sorted out."

"I'm sure we can get together then," Elaine said.

Adriana exclaimed, "I would be happy to meet at my house day after tomorrow. I will make all the arrangements for a lunch to be brought in." Then turning to Bonnie, she added, "A healthy lunch, of course, for our dietary needs. Mary, can you make a couple of your outstanding desserts?"

"Of course."

"Thank you, Adriana, for offering to host. I know we will work together to do something for Sabal Palms."

And just like that, the group had a new mission and a second wind.

Chapter Twenty-Two

Disgruntled as she left the town hall meeting, Shirley asked the investors, "Shall we go to my hotel, gentlemen, and put our heads together?"

The investors didn't wait that long. They began the discussion on the sidewalk outside the town hall meeting room as soon as the meeting ended.

Dinero turned to the other investors and asked, "Do you think this plan is salvageable? We will have to fight him all the way."

The look of fury on Green's face could not be mistaken. "Who does he think he is? Turning all holier-than-thou? Vowing to uphold *that* church? *That* faith? I thought we were all of the same mind. What happened to his commitment to our beliefs? To our concepts? How can he take it upon himself to fight our movement?"

Franklin added, "Not to mention trying to fight our money. Has he forgotten how deep our pockets are? Our combined worth? Does he now go against our movement to establish a new order in this country? One that supports beliefs other than Christianity? What about our other investments in other parts of the country? Will he go back on his word and try to destroy our other communities of New Age? He always told us the most important part of his community investments was decreasing Christian believers."

Green asked, "Yes, what did he always say? Distract, decrease, and disperse the Christians?"

"We can't stand for this!" Franklin's face turned red, and the veins in his forehead protruded.

"I'm going to ruin him!" Dinero declared. "And you all, you can help me."

Shirley was panicking. The investors were spiraling out of control. They were in a fit of rage. "Gentlemen, perhaps we should keep our eyes on this prize first."

Dinero said, "Shirley, you seem very calm under the circumstances. You just got fired—in public. You are now without a job."

"There's no question she knows her stuff. She knows *him*. She can probably guess his next move and, for that matter, all the moves he makes after that. I say, we get our heads together, name our group, and hire Shirley as our own assistant for this venture and others. We might need her for damage control on our previous investments," Green offered.

Relieved, Shirley waited to see if the others were on board with Green's suggested.

"Well, uh," Franklin uttered.

Shirley felt the knots building. What should she do? Proclaim things she wasn't sure she could do? She couldn't make promises about turning things around. She might not be able to fix this. She didn't want to give these investors false hope.

Franklin continued, "I think the only thing we need to do is ask Shirley her salary, then add ten percent."

Thank goodness, she thought.

"You're a tightwad. Let's make it twenty percent. I have faith that Shirley is just what we need to get the best of this . . . this traitor," Dinero suggested. "And if we get it worked out, she can keep the clause stating she will receive twenty-five percent of any net gain on the Sabal Palms project."

Shirley beamed. Maybe the failure of the first Sabal Palms proposal was just what she needed to make her mark.

"Gentlemen, I agree with Shirley's earlier suggestion. Let's go to her hotel, check in, and have a meeting to design our new proposal. I'm sure we will be able to get rooms on the island."

***

Trent took the hotel limo back across the causeway. His brain did not shut off for a second. He called his office in Miami and spoke to his second office assistant.

"Rose, this is Trent. Yes, fine, thank you. Recovering just fine. Look, about the Sabal Palms project, there have been some developments. Let's start at the beginning. Shirley Matthews is no longer with the company. Please pack up her belongings. Take security with you to observe your actions and then have the officer sign the necessary forms. Yes, Human Resources can assist you with the forms. Then you may text her and advise her to pick up her belongings when she returns to Miami. Next, you are promoted. You are now my personal assistant and will be paid accordingly. HR can help you with the transition and payroll forms for your raise. I will call them. You agreeable to this change in your position and role? . . . Good.

"Now, most important, I need you to scan and email every single page in the Sabal Palms file. I will also be in touch with Rodrigo about the accounting. I will let him know what I need, and please assist him in getting those documents to me. Yes, scan the ones he tells you to scan, and he will then ask to have some of the documents sent by courier on the next available flight. Better yet, ask him to bring them, and you can arrange for my plane to fly him over.

"Rose, listen carefully. I must have all documents and Rodrigo here by eleven a.m. day after tomorrow. Thank you."

Trent opened his hotel suite door and set the yellow tablet and binder on the conference room table. This would become his temporary Sabal Palms office. He called the front desk.

"Hello, Mr. Fortune. What can we do for you today?"

"Tell me, how long is this suite available?"

"We have no one requesting that room for another month."

"Perfect. Can you keep me in this suite until that date?"

"Of course. That will be four weeks from tomorrow."

"Thank you. And if you would, transfer me to room service. I will need a pot of coffee."

"Yes sir. I can order that for you, save you a call."

"Thank you. One last thing. Does the hotel have a printer that I can hook up here to use?"

"I can have one from the business center brought up."

"That would be fantastic. Thank you."

"No problem. Let me know if you need anything else."

Trent took a seat at the conference table. Now, he would dig in and figure out this problem. This is what he did best; he could put together an investment proposal from thin air. He had made his fortune doing so. This time, he would use his fortune to make a proposal of a lifetime.

***

The investors were impressed with the ride across the causeway. Green noted, "This is every bit as beautiful as Trent described. I am even more motivated to make this thing work."

Agreeing with Green's statement, Franklin said, "Perhaps we might even look around on the island for future investments."

Dinero nodded. "Great suggestion."

Shirley escorted the investors to the front desk of her hotel on the island. She waited for the clerk to finish a call about a reservation.

"May I help you, Miss Matthews?"

"Yes, these gentlemen each require a room for—how long do you think? A week?"

"Yes," Green said. "It may not take that long. We have done this quickly in the past."

Franklin and Dinero agreed.

"And do you have a conference room we can reserve for the same period of time?"

"We have a convention group coming in today, so let me check." She went to the computer and looked up the various conference room reservations. "It looks like there is only one conference room left open this week. It is pretty small, but let me ask. Will anyone else be joining you in this conference room?"

"No," Shirley replied. "It will just be the four of us."

"This will work then. I can give you each a key if you like."

"That would be good," Shirley said.

The clerk typed on the computer. "There. You are all set. Here are four keys to the Starfish Conference Room on the top floor. And, gentlemen, it will take me just a minute to get each of you set in a room. King bed suites okay?"

They all agreed.

In no time, the team of four checked into their rooms and set a meeting time. Each of the investors felt they could fight Trent. They did not understand that Trent, and the people from Sabal Palms, had their own Silent Partner.

***

The documents started arriving in Trent's email box before the printer was even hooked up in his private conference room. He spoke with his accountant, Rodrigo, and gave him instructions about the accounts and documents he needed. He talked with his company attorney, Susana, about how to liquidate his holdings in the converted churches across the country. There was a legal way to pull his money from the New Age organizations, and he would do so. It would not result in a large amount of money, but it would cause those organizations to scramble for money and possibly eventually fold altogether without his financial support.

Rodrigo agreed to send over the account information that Trent requested and to come to the meeting with the Sabal Palms group the day after tomorrow. Then Trent had another thought. What if he asked Susana to come along, too? The company might need legal representation to withdraw from the initial proposal. He didn't want to be caught off-guard. He called his new assistant, Rose, and asked her to arrange for Susana to fly to the meeting with Rodrigo.

The papers piled up in stacks. He printed off each document as it came. Within a few hours, his email inbox slowed, and he began to sort through the stacks of papers.

"I'm missing something. I don't see how to do this. I know there must be a way. It is probably right in front of my eyes."

He poured another cup of coffee. "I know what else I am missing. It's eight o'clock, and I haven't had dinner. That will give me a boost."

Room service was speedy. As usual, the fresh seafood was outstanding, and he felt renewed. He would work all night if needed. He had to find a way.

***

Shirley and the investors met promptly at three p.m. that same afternoon. One thing she knew from their reactions, they were determined to make this new proposal work.

"Shirley," Franklin began, "can you tell us anything about what led Trent to change his mind? Do you know? Did these people get to him after his crash? Did they take advantage of him?"

"Mr. Franklin, I will tell you I was taken by surprise. I arrived at the hospital shortly after Trent was rescued. As soon as I got there, I was told he wouldn't see me. He was only to have one visitor until he was moved."

"But why didn't you go to his room? You were by yourself," Green added.

"He already had one person in the ICU room with him. Later that same day, I met her—Elaine Smith."

Dinero leaned forward on the conference table. "I know that name. Isn't she the one we heard about last year? The one with, uh

. . . What was that crook's name? You know, that New York mobster. Oh! I know. Frankie the Gun. Somehow, this Elaine Smith got him to confess his crime of murder."

It was only then that Shirley put it all together. "*She* talked him into leaving New Age," she whispered.

"What?" Franklin asked.

"Look, if she could talk a criminal into confessing, she could talk Trent into leaving New Age. She caught him when he was vulnerable, maybe on pain pills or whatever. She went to his hospital room, and he was captive. He couldn't leave, and she talked to him about her faith. That has to be it."

Dinero spoke up. "It was more than that. He kept saying he had a second chance. People who nearly die say that. He must have thought he needed to pray or something—maybe he *did* pray before he was rescued. Then, when he was rescued, he attributed his rescue to his silly, little prayer."

Green added, "That scenario makes the most sense. But does he actually believe this rubbish? People who feel they had a second chance, well, it doesn't last. Look, remember that guy who came to our country club after he won that big lottery? He said he had a chance to start over. But what happened? You remember?"

Mr. Dinero said, "He went broke. He spent his money like he always did before, only he had way more to spend. Then, within six months, he'd spent it all."

"Exactly," Mr. Green said.

Shirley spoke up. "So, you are saying after a while, Trent will go back to New Age and to his usual money-making schemes?"

"I will bet on it. And when I bet on investments, I almost always win."

Puzzled, Shirley asked, "And if he does, what then? Do we let Trent back in on this deal?"

Gruffly, Franklin said, "No. Can't be trusted."

Dinero agreed. "I say he missed his chance. We are starting something new—something better, stronger. He is not invited."

But the investors underestimated the strength of Trent's faith and his God.

Chapter Twenty-Three

Trent worked all day the next day. No matter where he looked—no matter what account, or fund, or investment—he came up with the same conclusion: his funds were not enough. He would need help. It was now a matter of where and how to get the help he needed. He prayed his accountant and attorney would be able to brainstorm and develop a new plan.

He summoned the hotel limo to take him to the airport. He would take his attorney and his accountant to Sabal Palms. Following the meeting, they would go with him back to the island. He arranged for each of them to have a room at his same hotel. He believed God would make things clearer to him soon. He had faith.

"Hi, Trent," Susana said. "You look surprisingly well; you look pretty good. Not too many bruises."

"I agree," Rodrigo said. "We were so shocked when we heard about the crash. The entire company. We had prayer chains going; oh, I'm sorry. I know you don't believe in that kind of thing."

"You had prayer chains going? Really? For me? I think that is wonderful."

Susana and Rodrigo, shocked by his statement, were momentarily speechless.

"You do?" Susana timidly asked.

"Yes. I will tell you all about it. But maybe another time. Here is the short version. God gave me a second chance to start over. And this time, I want to do things the right way."

Then Rodrigo smiled. "That explains it."

"What?" Trent asked.

"Why you are liquidating your investments in the New Age buildings."

"Yes. I know it won't bring much money."

Confused, Rodrigo continued, "You don't know?"

"Know what?"

"Yesterday, you asked for your initial investment funding for those buildings."

"Yes, and you sent them. They aren't worth a lot of money."

"You really *don't* know. You turned some of those old churches into New Age coffee houses. Well, the truth is, the people who visit those coffee houses have no idea that they are connected to the New Age movement. They just thought it was pretty cool to go inside an old church and have a cup of coffee. Sure, there were a few New Age books on the shelves. But that wasn't the draw. I visited a few of them, and frankly, the books were never touched, only collecting dust. The customers just wanted a good cup of coffee. Those coffee shop locations, which happens to be ten of the fifteen church buildings, have been amazingly successful. They are worth twenty times your investment. And that is just the available cash revenue in our accounts," Rodrigo informed him. "The potential for continued revenue is astronomical."

"Seriously?"

Susana joined the conversation. "Yes. In fact, when Rodrigo told me what you wanted to do, to completely get out of those investments, I suggested a work-around kind of strategy."

Curious, Trent replied, "Which is?"

"We restructure those properties. The investors have a choice of buying you out at fifty times their investment—which, according to their net worth, they can't afford—or allowing you to restructure into a chain of coffee shops with no emphasis or connection to New Age. And in doing so, you refund their investment to buy them out. The other five churches, well, you can sell them to the investors if they want to continue."

"And if they don't want to keep them?"

"We offer a fair price and change them to be the same type of restructured coffee shops."

"I like it. I knew there was a reason I hired you." Trent laughed. "And with these new earnings, how much better shape am I in? I mean, compared to the amount of investment money needed to fund the Sabal Palms development?"

"You will still need a healthy sum. I can put a pencil and paper to it, given the new option of retaining those coffee shops."

"Rodrigo, I think I want to do more than just retain them. I think I want to turn them into family-friendly-type places, maybe with a playground outside and tables. And I want them to reflect Christian values and teaching."

"Good idea. I think the Christian community will be drawn to a place where they know their children will see good role models and Christian values."

Susana turned to Trent. "Can I ask you how committed you are to this development? And to Christianity?"

"As committed as I have ever been to anything. Even more so. This is why I am here, why I was given a second chance. I want to improve things, help people, rather than force some bizarre religion on them."

The three arrived at Adriana's house, and Trent introduced his attorney and his accountant to the group.

Adriana, in her usual flamboyant attire, jangling jewelry, and overpowering perfume, welcomed them into her home. She introduced them to Ramon, Maria, Billy, Mary, and Bonnie. She was about to introduce Elaine when Susana interrupted.

"And you must be Elaine? We have heard so much about you."

"Oh, my, well, my goodness, nice to meet you."

Rodrigo added, "Billy Wrangle, I am a huge fan."

"Thank you, sir."

"My stars! Let's go into the dining room. The table is large enough for us to all sit around it. Are we ready?"

"Past ready!" Bonnie said.

"For heaven's sake, I thought you would never ask," Mary said.

Ramon and Maria nodded, and the entire group was seated.

Trent began, "This group of people are not only fine citizens of Sabal Palms, but they represent the heartbeat. Bonnie, Elaine, Ramon, and Maria all live right along the shore. Adriana had a property that was on the chart to buy in the initial proposal, but she wants to stay right where she is and keep her entire property. And Mary, like Adriana, lives in town here. But Mary is in touch with the people who oversee the turtle rescue effort, the marine life protection effort, and the wildlife refuge. They all attend the little church on the shore. So, you see, they truly represent Sabal Palms.

"I heard a story about Sabal Palms when I visited the first time. These people, they all stick together. They all worked hard after the hurricane last year. They put this town back together. I know they are in touch with a man named Carlos. I met Carlos at Bonnie's house not long ago. I've been told Carlos can fix and build just about anything. He will be an invaluable contact for any future builds we might have here in Sabal Palms. I understand he repaired the church after the storm. We can ask for his help in our future plans.

"Now, to the matter at hand. My accountant and attorney have been researching a few areas of my company's investments. Rodrigo informed me this morning that we might be in a little bit better position than I assumed."

Rodrigo added, "Yes, the holdings of Evergreen Recreation and Conservation Industries have increased over the years. We are in a good position. Our net worth is strong. We can use this as leverage to seek a loan, or whatever means needed, to fund a project here at Sabal Palms."

Elaine was confused. She had hoped for better news. She had hoped the company would be able to fund any project in its entirety. She hesitated to ask, but she wanted to know. "Trent, is there any other way to raise funds? We were able to raise a modest amount within just a couple of days for possible attorney's fees."

"Oh? How much is a modest amount?"

"Billy put on a free concert here. We had a terrific turn-out, and within just a few hours that night and the next morning, we raised around twelve thousand dollars. It was just from people's pockets, really."

"What night was that?" Trent asked.

"The night your plane crashed."

"So, that is what I saw from the air. I saw the concert when I was flying over the island, and it was a great turnout."

Rodrigo's face lit up. "Elaine, that is a great idea. You've given me another approach."

"Rodrigo," Trent said, "we can't raise the funds we need by having a free concert."

"No, no. I am thinking of a different approach all the way around."

Mary was about to burst. "And? Tell us. Spill it."

Bonnie agreed. "If you have an answer to this problem, we need to know."

Ramon and Maria leaned in on the table and got their pencils ready to write down what Rodrigo was about to say.

Billy spoke up. "You know, I would be happy to have another concert if that is what you want to do."

Rodrigo continued. "Let me ask you fine folks. As a community, would you be interested in a joint venture?"

"Wait a minute. Antony—God rest his soul"—a pause again for the crossing of her chest—"said never get too many chefs in the kitchen."

"No, not too many," Rodrigo replied. "Just a small group of interested citizens who are willing to invest in, say, just the golf course. And then perhaps another small group would invest in just the beachside café. Another group, the inn. You get the picture? Spread the wealth around."

"And the cost," Mary was quick to add.

"Of course, the investment would be required to be a part of any or all of these ventures. Whoever wants in for specific properties. And the funds already collected for attorneys' fees, well, we can use that to address the cost of setting up the separate LLCs, uh, corporations."

Susana added, "I could do some of the work pro bono, and we can also outsource for the community so you would all share an outside attorney. And I would advise Trent from his business end. Your outside attorney would be careful with your own interests, and we would consult on all of the specifics."

The room was quiet once again. No one wanted to be the first to speak, but all were curious.

Again, Mary was first to ask. "Just how much are we talking about here?"

Rodrigo replied, "Each property would be a different amount. But just for an example. Let's pick a number to illustrate. Remember, I would have to look over all the appraisals and projections to make the actual amounts known to you. But for now, to clarify for understanding, let's just use the figure of one hundred dollars. Let's say Trent invests eighty percent or eighty dollars. Then the rest of you, whoever might be interested, would divide up the remaining portion. You can divide equally or decide how much of it you want to donate, and we can set it up as shares. Elaine might want five shares, and Bonnie ten, and so on. You would all be named to the board and weigh in on all decisions."

"And we each decide the amount and say which property we might want to help with? What if we can't come up with enough funds?"

Trent said, "We will see at that point what we might want to do. Maybe we decide to give up the inn until we can fund it with proceeds from the golf course. The point is, we would all agree to participate and pay as we can afford it. As it stands right now, I already own enough property to do what we want, except for the beachside café. That property we would need to purchase or go slow and purchase it in the future. It is up to the people in this room to decide."

Billy said, "Let me see if I understand correctly. Right now, you do not need the other investors to purchase any property. You just need additional funds for building the inn and the golf course for the development?"

"Yes, that is right."

Billy continued, "Then as long as you hold on to the property, those other investors from Miami can't intrude?"

"That is what I am telling you."

Relief filled the room.

Elaine asked, "Then our only need for development is to increase funding for the town of Sabal Palms for improvements?"

Trent answered, "Well, yes, and of course you would each make some type of profit eventually, once the golf course opened and the inn and so on."

Adriana threw up her arms and jangled her bracelets. "Yes! I am in all the way!"

Chapter Twenty-Four

Shirley and the investors called Trent and asked for another meeting to be held in the town hall meeting room of Sabal Palms. Trent was reluctant but checked with Elaine and the others, who were anxious to put this battle to rest. The meeting was set for the following morning. Elaine hoped it would not last long and that she would have the rest of the afternoon free to get some writing finished.

Elaine picked Bonnie up at nine o'clock, and they drove into town.

"After all this malarkey of the New Age people taking over our town is finally over, we should have a cookout at my place to celebrate."

"Terrific idea, Bonnie. How are you feeling about this meeting today?"

"Not really feeling anything. You?"

"Wondering if it's going to be a showdown or standoff or just a peaceful parting of the ways."

"Certainly a lot of different ways it could end. But the most important thing is, it is *ending*!

"Yes. And we can get back to our everyday routines. We can have swim parties at Adriana's again, and leisurely beach walks with no drones, and more cookouts."

"It all sounds like . . . fond, distant memories."

"We will be there again, Bonnie. You know we will. And soon."

***

The town meeting room was empty when Elaine and Bonnie arrived. They had been given instructions not to say anything to the investors. Trent wanted his attorney, accountant, or himself to handle the conversations with Shirley, Dinero, Franklin, and Green. Adriana, Mary, Ramon, Maria, and Billy dwindled in.

At last, Trent came in. "Good morning, all," he said. "I had a text from Shirley. They are just getting into Sabal Palms from the island."

A turn of the handle of the door was followed by the clattering footsteps of the others from Miami.

Shirley nodded. "Trent, how are you? Looks like the recovery has gone well."

"Yes, thanks. I am great. Gentlemen." He nodded.

Shirley asked, "Would you like to speak first, or shall we move forward with our proposal?"

"Oh, please, go right ahead," Trent said.

Franklin started first. "Trent, we have put our heads together, and we came up with a plan that we think we can all live with. And we ran the numbers and took Shirley's recommendations to heart. I think you will be pleased with the projected earnings."

Trent looked at the investors from Miami and then at Shirley.

He really has a great poker face, Elaine thought. *They have no clue what we are up to.*

Trent nodded. The investors each took turns presenting one section after another. Shirley put charts up on an easel and pointed. She yammered on, all the while, displaying an abundance of confidence.

After nearly two hours, the Miami group was finished. The bottom line, as far as Elaine could tell, was that they wanted to move forward with the plans as Shirley had revised. There would be no changes in property lines, no privacy for the beach homeowners, and no consideration for keeping the Christian church a Christian church. In summary, it was an even greedier proposal than the original one.

Trent addressed the group. "While we appreciate all of the time you have put in for the proposal for Sabal Palms, we unequivocally reject it."

Shirley gasped; Franklin's vein popped out on his forehead; Green's face turned red; and Dinero grunted.

Shirley protested, "What do you mean? You can't be serious."

"I am totally serious."

Franklin huffed, "You're out of your mind. You can't fund this without a great deal more money!"

Green said, "You need us, Trent."

Dinero agreed. "Yes. You cannot do it alone."

"On the contrary, I don't need your money. Remember that I already own the property needed to further these plans."

"And what about the funding for development? Who is going to put up that money?"

"These wonderful people," Trent said.

Shirley laughed. "Really? You're kidding, right?"

Susana spoke up. "We have formed an LLC joint venture for the golf course, the inn, and so on. All funding is secured."

The Miami group continued with their huffing and puffing and bloviating for another thirty minutes. They couldn't believe they were out of the picture completely.

When all had calmed down, Trent said, "Just a couple of other items of business. My attorney and accountant have contacted your offices and submitted the revised plans for the additional New Age properties across the country. Your people have agreed to consider—and, in fact, thought the ideas were sound—to remove your interests in those properties. It will bring you all some additional funds, which your people tell me you need. Your investments were small, and you accountants believe these funds I am suggesting to you for the properties will clear up all loans you had for the properties."

"What? You are buying us out?" Dinero asked.

"Yes. Your initial investment and your share in the business are insignificant. These properties will become Christian-based, family coffee houses. If you do not go along with my buying back your interests, just know that since I hold the majority of interest, these businesses will now be Christian-based establishments."

A variety of sounds were emitted quickly by the Miami investors. When they quieted, Shirley said, "If there is nothing further . . . "

"Wait, there is one more thing," Trent added. "It has become clear to me over the last several days that we had the wrong approach in our business ventures. Investing should not be about taking advantage of people. It should be about working together to make these towns, this countryside—wherever you invest—a better place. And there is something else. Whether you know it or not and whether you like it or not, God's army is strong. There are more Christian soldiers out there than you can possibly imagine. And they, like the people of Sabal Palms, will not back down to the New Age beliefs and practices. In fact, I will personally lead a campaign against any weakening of Christian values and any misinterpretation of Scripture. And finally, know this—and I mean this with all sincerity—I will be praying for you all."

Angrily, the Miami investors stood and left the room.

"Wow!" Bonnie said. "That was outstanding!"

"Touchdown!" Mary yelled.

"Yes! Yes! Yes!" Adriana cheered.

Ramon and Billy shook Trent's and Rodrigo's hands. Maria hugged them both. Susana hugged everyone from Sabal Palms.

After they had settled down a bit, Trent said, "I am hosting a celebration dinner in my suite tonight. Five-thirty. I expect you all to come. I have arranged for us to have our own private buffet served by the head chef. From here on out, I see great things for our future. Blessed events. Blessed ventures."

"Sounds amazing," Elaine said.

***

Elaine and Bonnie headed back to their beach cottages and the others to their respective homes. They made plans to go to the island in two cars. They would meet at Mary's house at five o'clock and ride together. It would be a true celebration of great food and fellowship. Sabal Palms would be back on track.

Back in his hotel, Trent sat in his living room of the penthouse suite. He looked out over the gulf and said a prayer. Then, he picked up his cell phone and dialed. The phone rang on the other end.

"Mom?"

"Is this Trent? Are you okay? My, it's been—"

"Too long."

"Yes, too long. But, I saw on the news . . . Are you okay? Your plane . . . "

"Yes, Mom, I'm fine. I am calling because, Mom, I want to come home. I want to see you and Dad."

"Really?" She began to sob. "Oh, Trent . . . "

"Would next week be okay with you?"

She sniffled. "Trent, next week would be perfect."

"I have so much to tell you. I love you, Mom, and please tell Dad I love him."

***

The dinner at the penthouse suite had been incredible. Elaine had never seen such a display of delicious foods. But she was glad to be home. She was thankful the threat to Sabal Palms had ended. She put her comfy clothes on and sat before her typewriter. She reflected on the good friends she had in Sabal Palms. She thought about Trent's change of heart and how he had been rescued right out of the claws of death by God Himself. She was amazed at God's glory and His blessings.

Elaine knew she would soon be writing songs again with Billy Wrangle. She would participate in a well-thought-out plan for helping Sabal Palms generate money and improve the community. She looked forward to the hiring of a new Christian pastor. Indeed, a lot to look forward to in her life.

Momentarily, it crossed her mind how much she cherished living on the shore and being near God's power of the sea. She looked at Bella, content in her bed. Contentment. Nice. A good feeling. Then she glanced at her calendar. November. Hurricane season would be over soon. And then, in a mere month, it would be Christmas in Sabal Palms. She smiled.

She rolled the paper in the typewriter. Her fingers typed out, "Peace isn't just the absence of problems. We now are free from problems at Sabal Palms. But it is more than that. We find peace only with God."

Then she opened her Bible to Romans 14:19 and read, "So then let us pursue what makes for peace and for mutual upbuilding."

"And that is just what we will do," she whispered.

Next in the *Sabal Palms* series . . .

Terry Overton

Christmas *at*
Sabal Palms

Sabal Palms
A NOVELLA

For more information about
Terry Overton
and
Sabal Palms After the Storm
please visit:

www.terryovertonbooks.com
www.facebook.com/allthingspossiblewithhim
@terryoverton6

Ambassador International's mission is to magnify the Lord Jesus Christ
and promote His Gospel through the written word.

We believe through the publication of Christian literature, Jesus Christ and
His Word will be exalted, believers will be strengthened in their walk with
Him, and the lost will be directed to Jesus Christ as the only way of salvation.

For more information about
AMBASSADOR INTERNATIONAL
please visit:

www.ambassador-international.com
@AmbassadorIntl
www.facebook.com/AmbassadorIntl

More from Ambassador International

When Dr. Sam Gray is sent to Africa as a volunteer physician, he is counting down the days until he can go home again. During a trip to the local school, he runs into the Cloverdales, a missionary family determined to win every soul in Africa to Christ. Try as he might, Dr. Sam can't seem to resist the family and finds himself being pulled into their midst again and again. As he battles his own beliefs, Dr. Sam begins to find that maybe he's in need of a Physician as well. Can anyone heal his hardened heart?

When Addy and her sister Molly step off the Orphan Train Steamer in Ephraim, Wisconsin, no one waits for them. Hopes for a family that would treat them kindly are gone. Addy determines to find a job and care for her sister, but that presents problems she can't quite handle. Join Addy in her quest to grow into the heritage of the islanders by becoming a strong survivor and helping others do the same. Her attitude and actions will delight you and drive you crazy.

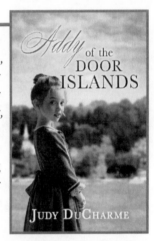

After his wife dies, Marco finds himself lonely and desperate for companionship. Katie is an abused woman, who is now tied to caring for an invalid husband. When Marco and Katie meet, they form a bond quickly. Realizing they are walking a line outside of God's will, Marco returns to his life in New York with Katie telling him to forget her forever. But she is never far from his mind. Does God bring beauty from ashes? Can God repair what has been broken and "make all things new"?